A Victorian Justice

by

Patricia C. Behnke

Patricia C. Behnke

Dry Bones Press
Roseville, California

A Victorian Justice
by Patricia C. Behnke

Dry Bones Press, Inc.
P. O. Box 597
Roseville, CA 95678

(415) 707–2129
http://www.drybones.com/

Publisher's Cataloging–in–Publication Information
FICTION
Behnke, Patricia C. Dec. 23, 1954 —
A Victorian Justice / by P. Behnke
New Voices in American Fiction: Mystery series
p.   cm.
1–883938–82–1
I. Author   II. Title

CHAPTER ONE

February 1980

"I wonder what she's doing tonight?" Hollis Canon thought as he locked the door on Canon Furniture Store on Main Street. For a brief moment he pictured May Randall standing before him beckoning him to the back door of the furniture store.

The late afternoon shadows deepened as Hollis turned to begin the walk to his home only three blocks away shaking away the vision of May from his mind. The evening air, cold and brisk with a tendency to freeze nostril hair if breathing too deeply, held the hint of snow.

Even though the Canon family had owned the store since the 1800s, this particular storefront had been rebuilt eight years ago after a devastating fire. Its new front did not detract from the one hundred year old storefronts next door since it had been rebuilt to look exactly like the old building. Only upon close inspection could it be detected that the furniture store's Victorian facade contained new windows and trim.

As he often did, he thought back to that night over eight years ago and wondered about May Randall. Once again he looked up at the stars brightly shining over this small Michigan town and wondered if May could be looking at the same sky thinking of him. He sadly shook his head and tried desperately not to remember the beauty of his wife's sister as she made sweet love to him one last time on the couch in the office of the old furniture store the night of the fire.

He turned toward Canon Funeral Home and his own house sitting behind it trying to block thoughts of May from his mind. He hoped that there would be no calls tonight for him to embalm a body because May's memory lingered even in the embalming room in the basement of the funeral home where they had first made love, and he

3

knew it would take prodigious amounts of whiskey to drive away the demons on this bitter cold February night.

Hollis also owned and operated the only local funeral home in Victoria, Michigan, but it had been a slow month for funerals. The embalming of bodies kept him drunk most of the time, and memories of May made it even worse.

He walked carefully through the slush almost refrozen from the day's slight warming trend. Light ice edged each puddle, making the liquid very cold and uncomfortable on pant legs. He looked across the street to the village square and noticed that the town hall with its turrets and brick face seemed to offer shelter and protection to its citizens as the town's fortress. But it hadn't been able to protect him against the cataclysm of his life eight years ago when he had allowed the only woman he had ever loved to slip away past the town's limits and out of Victoria forever.

As Hollis crossed Center Street, he noticed a police car cruising slowly around the corner. It pulled parallel to the curb of the sidewalk.

"Sir, aren't you Hollis Canon?" said a voice from the passenger's window of the car.

"Yes, that's right, officer. Is there a problem?"

"No, no problem, Mr. Canon. You probably don't remember me, but I'm Evert's son, Chuck. I went to school with Tom."

"Of course, Chuck! I heard you were made detective last year. It's good to see you. Tom, you know, is teaching at Iowa State. I'll be sure to tell him I saw you the next time we talk."

"That would be fine, Mr. Canon. Tell him I said 'Hi' and that we'll have to get together the next time he comes home." Chuck opened his door and climbed out to shake Hollis' hand.

"I was also interested in finding out about your daughter, Beverly. Does she still live around here?" Chuck asked.

"Well, Beverly lives in Ann Arbor now. She's getting married next summer. But Beverly was quite a bit younger than you, wasn't she? Why are you interested in her?"

"It's police business, Sir. Now don't get upset, Beverly's

4

done nothing wrong, far from it. We were hoping she could help us."

"Yes, go on," Hollis Canon said now more warily.

"Well, now, it may be difficult for you to hear what I have to say, and I could just talk to Beverly and not bother you, if you could just tell me how to find her."

"Chuck, whatever it is, I would like to know. Why don't you tell me what it is, and then I'll call her. I know you can locate her on your own, but this might be better, don't you think?"

"All right, Mr. Canon, I can appreciate that, and yes, I agree, I think it might be better this way." Chuck now paused not quite sure how to proceed. He had known Hollis Canon for as long as he could remember, and he did not want to make him uncomfortable.

"When Beverly was in high school, I believe she dated a James Kelly?"

Hollis' head jerked back in one swift motion. "Ah, yes, but that was a long time ago," he muttered rather lamely.

"Well, I don't mean to bring up bad memories, but we have heard from several sources that Beverly had a rough time with James. Several people have told us that he used to hit her when they were together. We've also have heard about other things." Chuck hurriedly took a breath.

"I only bring these things up because now James is being charged for severely beating and raping a young woman. She's sufficiently recovered from her wounds to press charges. Many character witnesses have been called: Coach Hoover, the Browns, Principal Mayer. They all have agreed to testify in James's defense, and there is a good chance he'll get off. I would hate to see that happen, Mr. Canon. My partner and I were out on another case that night, and found her in the road where her attacker left her. She knew James and identified him without a doubt as her attacker. And they were seen leaving a party together." Chuck paused again for a breath and reaction.

"Yes, I've read about all that business in the papers, and it doesn't surprise me one bit. But what's Beverly's connection?"

5

"We want her to testify for the prosecution that James Kelly is without a doubt capable of committing this crime."

"I'll call Beverly," said Hollis quietly.

Dusk settled on Ann Arbor as Beverly Canon unlocked her front door. She had two things on her mind: taking a hot bath and meeting her boyfriend later at the bar where he worked as a bartender. She almost ignored the insistently ringing phone as she came into her apartment; but she did answer it, in case it was Danny.

"Hello. Oh hi, Dad. No, I just came in the door. What's up?" Beverly knew something had to be wrong because her father never phoned; her mother was usually left to do phone calling if necessary.

"You remember Chuck Ward, Beverly?" her father began.

"Yeah, he was a couple of years older than me. Around Tom's age. Didn't they graduate together?"

"That's right. Well, he's a detective for the Ingham County Sheriff's office, and he stopped me tonight on my way home from work. He wanted to discuss his most current case; one in which he wants desperately to get a conviction." Hollis knew he was stalling, but it had been years since Beverly and he had discussed James Kelly, and then they never discussed him; they yelled about him.

"That's nice, Dad. He's got a great job, fine. What do you want?" Beverly asked impatiently thinking more of Danny than Chuck Ward.

"I'm trying to tell you, Beverly. Chuck's trying to convict James Kelly of rape and assault on a young girl who almost died after leaving a party with him. Chuck is certain James committed the crime, but he is afraid he will get off because certain citizens in Victoria like Bill Hoover are going to testify on his behalf, telling the jury what a fine decent young man he always was and that he simply is incapable of committing such a crime."

"I bet this makes you pretty happy, huh, Dad?"

"Of course not. But it's nothing more than I expected. Chuck wants you to testify for the prosecution."

"Testify to what?" was Beverly's angry reply.

6

"Testify that you know perfectly well that James is capable of doing what he did to that young girl."

"That's what you and Chuck think?"

"Beverly, what about you? You can't mean to say you are sticking up for that bastard?" Hollis was about to lose his temper with his only daughter.

"You never did understand, did you? You certainly didn't then, why would I expect you to now. What about what you are capable of doing? Don't talk to me about putting him away when you need to be sharing the same cell." Beverly was losing her control now that the whole issue had been opened up for the first time in nine years.

"Beverly, I don't understand you. I think he brainwashed you. What's wrong with you?" The anger was gone from Hollis' voice; all that remained was a definite sadness and longing for the daughter he once had.

"He did not brainwash me. You and the rest of Victoria are as much to blame for the rape of this girl as he is."

"I don't believe you! Why do you want to hurt your mother and me? We did everything we could for you. James is a bad seed, and we didn't want you involved with him. Period."

"Save it, Dad. You may lie to yourself, but don't try it with me. Are you forgetting about Aunt May? Are you forgetting about Coach Hoover who fooled around with all the young girls in his office while lecturing James about staying away from me? None of you wanted me involved with him because he was black. That's the 'period'."

"I can't talk to you anymore. You're not listening, and you have distorted this whole thing. What did we ever do to deserve this kind of treatment?"

"You know the answer to that as well as I do. I'm hanging up now. There's nothing more to discuss."

As she hung up the phone, the whole phantasm of eight years ago came rushing back in one great wave. She had kept it buried all this time in hopes it would go away. She knew one thing for certain as she fought to keep the dark void of those years from engulfing her. She would have to tell Danny.

If he truly wanted to marry her, and he said he did, he would have to hear everything, tonight; it wasn't fair to keep something so vital from him. And she hoped he would help to pull her up out of the nightmare of her past.

CHAPTER TWO

Autumn – 1970

Beverly Canon walked slowly home from school with a slight smile on her lips. Her hands grazed every shrub next to the sidewalk. Her thoughts centered on James Kelly and the way he looked at her as he walked by her today in the halls at school. The brilliant reds and oranges and yellows of the trees all around her as the Michigan autumn blossomed in full color could have been a million miles away for all she noticed.

James had playfully grabbed the end of the scarf she had worn around her neck that day and ran away pulling the scarf from her neck. He loped easily down the hall looking back over his shoulder with a playful grin splashed across his face. Laughing she had chased after him until she reached him.

"You should be more careful with your belongings, little girl." He grinned as he reached down and placed the scarf gently around her neck.

"Be careful about guys like you, you mean," she had responded matching his grin and looking up into his face over a foot away from hers.

He wore his pants low on his hips with his paisley shirt tucked in neatly under his varsity jacket. James at 6'8" towered over Beverly whose height hadn't yet reached 5'4". They both stood admiring each other for a few moments. When Beverly walked away she knew James was watching her as she swung her hips making the pleats on her very short blue skirt swing back and forth across her legs.

James had just started going to Victoria High last year as a sophomore. Beverly, a freshman, had watched James play basketball last year as he took the team to its first regional championship. Beverly, the only daughter in her family, had enjoyed watching her

9

talented and athletic brothers set records at VHS so she appreciated James' talent and had cheered for him when he played football this year. Now she looked forward to the new basketball season.

One day during the previous year, Beverly had approached James while he stood in line at the lunch counter.

"Hi, James? I'm Beverly Canon. I just wanted to tell you that I think you're very talented," she said in one breath.

"Uh, thanks. Canon? Related to Tom Canon?"

"My brother. He was good, but you're better."

James threw back his head and laughed deeply. "Thanks, Beverly. That's a compliment coming from a Canon."

James had admired and watched Beverly ever since that day. Most of the people who did bother to talk to him in Victoria did so for their own benefit, not because they wanted to tell him something sincerely.

James lived at Ravens Wood Lake, a small community fifteen miles southeast of Victoria. Not one single black person lived within the community of Victoria or any of the other small communities in the area.

Ravens Wood Lake lay just 50 miles from Detroit keeping and confining some of the members of Michigan's black community who had migrated from the South in the 1930s and more recently, from Detroit, the automobile factory capital of the country. By 1970, approximately one hundred blacks congregated in this loosely–knit village with no store, post office, library, or school.

The dirt main road through Ravens Wood passed clapboard houses grouped close to the road as it wound its way down to the small lake. The tall grasses surrounding it made a marshy playground for the children and a prime fishing spot for everyone.

The nearby town of Victoria drew many white professionals from Ann Arbor and Detroit who hoped to keep their town white. As a result, the citizens of Victoria had little contact with blacks except for the few bused in from Ravens Wood Lake. The black students went to the various schools near them based on what they had to offer a particular school. Any black student without a special talent would most often go to the poorest community.

Even though contact with blacks remained minimal, many white families from the area drove to Detroit to visit car shows at Cobo Hall or see the holiday decorations along the riverfront with their car windows rolled up and doors locked through the inner city streets while pointing to the blacks on the sidewalks and in the doorways of abandoned buildings.

"See, they're not much different from us," fathers and mothers whispered to their children, adding in a lower voice, "Be sure to keep your doors locked."

Michigan, covered with snow and sleet for nearly five months during the winter, left nothing much to do between the months of November and April. The major activity that incited and enhanced the imaginations of its citizens in the snowdrifts centered around the exciting games of basketball played on the local high school courts. Victoria, the smallest and most insipid of the area towns, had the most vigorous fans for winter sports.

Wooing by the high school coaches who cruised the dirt streets of Ravens Wood Lake brought the only blacks to the area schools which included Victoria. No one questioned this practice because nothing was more important than winning. Victoria's parents made sure their coaches wooed the hardest and loudest, therefore assuring that the black athletes of substance would attend Victoria High School.

Within the confines of Ravens Wood Lake, black southern traditions remained preserved. Hospitality prevailed in all homes. Greens and beans could be smelled from the doorways. The coaches who cruised the streets in the summertime, could be assured of the conviviality of the matriarchs cooking away in the small cramped kitchen quarters of most of these homes.

The dirt streets became the playground for the children. The adult males of Ravens Wood worked long hours in Detroit or Ypsilanti in the multitude of automobile factories and faced an hour's drive back home each evening. For them, the trade–off was worth it. They had created their own community. Their hopes and dreams for their children were no different from their white collar counterparts in Victoria; both groups of fathers knew they left their children each day with a safe place to play away from the drug dealers, murderers, thieves and the big city crimes of the ghetto that is Detroit.

James Kelly, the most visible resident of Ravens Wood Lake, caught Victoria's basketball coach Bill Hoover's eyes immediately. His height set him apart physically in many ways. At 6'7" and fifteen years old, he towered above his peers and turned all the coaches' heads on their first recruiting drive–through the summer of 1969.

Most of the coaches had been watching James, but it wasn't until he reached his phenomenal height that Bill Hoover paid close attention. James had gone to Chelsea High School during his freshman year, but Hoover spent an extraordinary amount of time at Ravens Wood that summer trying to recruit him for VHS. He ate with the Kellys and even kept his little dalliances with the high school girls to a minimum as he gave it his all in recruiting James.

"Hey, James Kelly, right?" Coach called from his Thunderbird one afternoon during a summer drive–through.

"Yeah, that's me." James turned around slowly to look at which coach it might be this time.

"Bill Hoover, Victoria High," he said as he got out of his car and came toward James with his outstretched hand.

"Coach," James said with little commitment.

"Now how'd ya like to come play with me and my boys this year, James? We've got a good chance at winning regionals, and with you, we might go all the way." Coach winked at James.

Bill Hoover had only been coaching and teaching for five years. His win/loss record looked good, but he wanted more. He wanted to win the state basketball championship. He didn't plan on staying in Victoria forever, and if it meant putting on a show for James and his mother than he could do it.

James's attitude remained cautious as he talked to Bill Hoover. He saw the Victorian coach as a way out and up for him so

12

he tolerated his obsequious behavior. However, he still remembered Stella's experience in Victoria.

His older sister, Stella, had attended Victoria High a few years earlier during the mid–1960s. She was the first black to attend VHS, and for her it was a lonely existence; one she survived by having a finely–tuned sense of humor. She made hordes of acquaintances as a result, but no invitations came for dinner. However, she provided status of sorts for those students who were friendly because they could always state proudly, "Oh, one of my best friends is black." Only this best friend didn't come over for dinner.

The invitations to dinner did come after her performance in the senior production of *Finian's Rainbow* when she stole the show by shuffling across the stage saying, "Here's your mint julep, Surrah." The more she shuffled, the louder the laughter and applause. She delighted the audience by acting out a role understood by them all.

Their acceptance came a little too late for Stella and for the wrong reasons. She graduated from VHS and was never heard from again in Victoria. No one remembered her name; but her shuffle remained indelibly inked on the town's collective memory. However, Stella knew that her acceptance came when she acted out an expected role, and James knew it, too.

As the coaches strained their necks out the windows of their Thunderbirds and Mustangs to glimpse his play at the local hoops, he had an inkling that he might prove to be the exception in his community.   He might actually have a chance at making it. And he thought Coach Hoover might provide the best vehicle since he had the best coaching record in the area.

So Bill Hoover successfully recruited, and James started as the center on the varsity team during the '69–70 season. When James came to VHS, no one objected especially after they had seen him play. They had seen him push in shot after shot of his less talented white teammates. They had seen James rebound for failed shots. They had seen James win games and take their high school basketball team to the regionals for the first time in twenty years, and

13

he was only a sophomore.

Spirits and bets soared as everyone realized James had not yet hit his peak. Moreover, if James stayed at VHS those two years of peaking court time would result in a state championship for the entertainment–starved town of Victoria.

Suddenly at fifteen James was a minor celebrity, and everyone was happy. James received applause for finally putting Victoria on the map with write–ups in all of the state's major newspapers. He had even been named to the All State first string basketball team.

Winter had never been so lively in this small community. The local grocery store owners won all their bets, and they wore smiles. Everyone was happy; everyone except maybe for James and his mother who realized all the articles in the papers rang slightly false as they praised Victoria for its liberal attitudes.

Yes, James attended school in Victoria, he won games for them and even used the same locker room as everyone else, and he was the star at the end–of–the–year banquet, but there it ended. The invitations never came once the basketball season ended that first year. But no one noticed or cared in Victoria. However, James at sixteen was just beginning to come into his manhood that year when he turned into a star. And he cared.

Beverly continued her walk down the street thinking of nothing but James' wide smile and dark face, and she found she cared, too. She wanted to see more of him and smiled to herself as she thought how it might feel to kiss his lips much larger than her own. She became short of breath just thinking of it. She walked past all the other store fronts on Main Street oblivious to anything but thoughts of James Kelly.

She entered Canon Furniture Store as Karen Adams put the finishing touches on a window display of end tables and lamps.

"Hey, Karen, what's up?"

"Hi, Beverly. Not much," Karen answered as she jumped down from the window display.

Karen and Beverly made a stark contrast with one another. Karen's curves looked almost cheap next to Beverly's thin, delicate build. Karen's dark eyes, outlined in dark brown, created a far older look than Beverly with her startling ice blue eyes and blonde hair. Beverly wore a light blue sweater and matching mini–skirt by Bobbie Brooks while Karen wore a simple white blouse with a peter pan collar which looked as if it had seen better days. Karen's clothes always seemed to be a size too small as they strained to fit over her voluptuous seventeen year old body.

"How come you're not in study hall anymore?" Beverly asked. She and Karen were two years apart in school but since Karen had been working at the store, the two had become friendly.

"I started working as Coach Hoover's aide last month."

"Ah, well, be careful. I hear he takes on a new girl every year," Beverly said half–teasing.

"Oh, right." Karen quickly turned away so Beverly wouldn't see her blush or the uncontrollable smirk form on her lips.

"Where's my dad? In the office?" Beverly headed for the back of the store.

"I think so. I saw your Aunt May come in a little while ago, and they went toward the back. She seemed upset."

"Probably Uncle Johnny beat the you–know–what out of her again. I probably shouldn't interrupt. Just tell my dad I stopped by to see if he was ready to walk home."

"Oh, sure, Beverly. See ya later." As soon as Beverly left the store, Karen headed for the phone on the counter.

"Bill, I work until 5:30 tonight. No, that's OK. I'll meet ya there." Karen slowly set the receiver back on the phone and smiled as she thought about her date with the basketball coach later that night.

CHAPTER THREE

The next day at school, James stopped by Beverly's locker for a minute between classes. They stood there talking before the tardy bell rang for the next class.

"Are you going to the opening game tomorrow night?" James asked casually as he draped his arm over the top of Beverly's locker.

"Sure, I wouldn't miss it! I know this year you're going to take us all the way to state, James," Beverly said as she smiled up into his face.

"Good, I'll see ya there. Maybe I'll see ya later at the dance, too," James ventured to see how she would react.

"You better save at least one victory dance for me," she said laughing.

Beverly floated to her next class as she imagined dancing with James Kelly. She thought that he would be a very graceful dancer just from the way he lithely dribbled the ball, casually moving down the court as if the two guards surrounding him simply didn't exist.

As Beverly and her best friend Laura walked home from school that afternoon, Beverly related the conversation with James.

"You told him to save you a dance? He is kind of cute, but what will everyone think?" Laura asked innocently.

"What do you mean?"

"Well, he's black, Beverly."

"Oh, really? So what?" Beverly stopped on the corner of her block to look at her friend aghast.

"You know how this town is. My god, Beverly, your family practically invented the rules. Don't tell me you don't know what I'm talking about," Laura said defensively.

"Well, my parents aren't that way and as for everyone else,

16

who cares? It's just a dance, and he's a nice guy. I feel sorry for him because he really doesn't have any good friends here. I'd be lost if I didn't have you to talk to, so imagine how it must be for James." Beverly looked sadly at Laura.

"I know, and he is nice, but I know this town and so do you, Bev, so be careful," Laura warned one last time.

The girls had just come to Center Street where Beverly lived. On the corner opposite them was the small Baptist Church with its small steeple and peeling paint near the front door.

At the other end of the block facing Main Street, stood the majestic Presbyterian Church with its much taller steeple and stained glass windows at every opening even in the port holes of the front door.

Continuing down Elizabeth Street in the next block stood the square, stoic steeple of the Methodist Church. The side windows of the chapel area were stained glass but everything else at the Methodist Church spoke of restraint and unpretentious simplicity.

Beverly looked closer at the white starkness of her church, one of the mainstays of this community. She had been born into the upper echelon of the Methodist Church and its tightly held community. The church had taught her strict definitions and guidelines regarding the other religions and churches.

According to those closest to Beverly, the Methodists had somehow been THE CHURCH and all others fell short in some way and always that shortcoming would be pointed out whenever another church or a member of that other church was mentioned. Beverly remained confused, however, as to who said and did and decided all these things. She learned early on to never question, especially when the nostrils of the family's elders began alternately pinching and flaring. The only way to tell how strongly a Methodist felt was to watch the nostrils; they gave it all away.

Beverly's confusion deepened one night when she found her father passed out over a dead body in the embalming room in the basement of the funeral home. When she saw the empty bottle of whiskey next to him on the floor, she knew better than to ask her

17

mother any questions. The next morning Martha Canon looked at her husband in disdain when he stumbled in the back door of his home after sleeping it off at the funeral home. Martha Canon's nostrils silenced Beverly's unasked and unanswered questions.

The Methodists and the other Protestant churches had their own classifications for everyone and everything within their own small orbit. Anyone drifting out of the definitions risked ostracism from all. However, if those deviances remained hidden and buried, all heads turned in the other direction and ignored what didn't come to light. Hence, everyone suspected that Hollis Canon drank, but because he never revealed it publicly, everyone went about the serious business of ignoring it.

And just because Johnny Randall cheated on his wife, May, and May, Beverly's aunt, indulged in her own secret life, no one bothered them because they didn't make a spectacle of themselves. The facade of normalcy was all that mattered to a good Methodist.

The Presbyterians, the closest in doctrine and feeling to the Methodists, had one distinct difference because the members of this church were RICH. In the world of a Methodist the word "rich" could be said to be synonymous with evil.

One day Beverly overheard her mother talking with a neighbor and heard the distinction well enough.

"Well, you know about the educational wing, don't you?" Martha Canon asked Doris Stanhope.

"Educational wing? That's what they call it? Let's call it what it is: an extravagant waste of money thrown in our face!" Doris replied flaring and pinching in indignation.

"They certainly like to let the rest of us know they're rich, don't they?" Martha almost whispered this pronouncement although emphasizing harshly the word "rich".

Actually in 1965, the Presbyterians had built a modern educational wing and let the community use it for various activities, free of charge. The Methodist members ignored the existence of this wing for two years even though it faced the front of the Methodist Church.

When one of Beverly's uncles decided to hold a wedding anniversary reception there, many nostrils were pinching and flaring in the Canon family, but the large unit of aunts and uncles attended, and it seemed finally the Methodists had come down off the mountain and acknowledged the brotherhood of their fellow Christians. In fact, so much so, that from 1968 on, in the summers, they took turns worshipping at each other's church so the ministers could each have a summer month off. However, the Presbyterians were still rich, and the Methodists took comfort in their middle class suffering.

Protestant churches were the only ones allowed within the town limits of Victoria. About ten miles out in the country, that other church resided. The townspeople knew who belonged to that church because the names of those members were not mentioned without their religious affiliation following behind. For example, a true Protestant Victorian would say, "Yes, I know Al Johnson, the Catholic."

The Catholics, touted as "godless" creatures, even allowed dancing, drinking, and card playing in the basement, right underneath the place of worship. Even the Presbyterians confined those activities to the basements of certain church members' homes. Some were even so bold as to say the Mafia controlled Mount Holly Catholic Church. Where else would all the gold and silver and jewels come from?

A family of Catholics lived on the same street as Beverly, and all the neighborhood ills were blamed on them. They had five kids, all under the age of ten, so extraordinary amounts of blaming took place. And Beverly's mother wasted no words when it came to those children.

Martha Canon often told her daughter, "You are not allowed to play with them under any circumstance."

Since no other children Beverly's age lived in the neighborhood, inevitably they would find ways to play together, and they did.

When Beverly was five she was caught exploring with one of the boys from "that" family. However, there was no question as to blame in the garage that day when Beverly's mom opened the side

19

door and saw two five year olds with their pants down. Beverly was soundly spanked, for disobeying her directive about playing with "those" children, and hauled into the house where Beverly heard further rantings on the evils of Catholics.

Her mother became convinced her daughter could not have thought of that behavior on her own. It was convenient for everyone that the little boy with whom Beverly chose to experiment was Catholic. Beverly's mother loved scapegoats especially when it came to exonerating her own children.

Beverly's brother George, ten years older than Beverly, seemed to be an unlikely candidate to test his parent's prejudices. George remained a very shy, introverted teenager with only an interest in playing sports even after going away to college. He never had the nerve to ask any girl out on a date.

In George's junior year of college, he came home for the holidays and finally consented to let his younger brother, Dave, fix him up with a girl from high school. Susan was a nice, cute girl, but George would have fallen for anyone on that first successful date at twenty–one.

One date led to another and Susan ingratiated herself into the family, or so it seemed on the surface. She had a tremendous black mark against her, and it had not yet presented itself for discussion in the family. She was, "Susan, the Catholic."

One day at Sunday dinner with a table laden with an over-abundance of food, George broke the news to his parents.

"Mom, Dad, I've asked Susan to marry me," he finally blurted.

"Oh, George, that's wonderful! Susan is a wonderful girl, and once she becomes confirmed everything will be fine," Martha gushed as she went to George and gave him a hug. She had never confessed to anyone that she had been slightly worried that George never left the house much when he was home and seemed content to spend most of his time with her.

"George, congratulations," Hollis said. He looked at his son with pride. George had also worried him. As tall as Hollis and equally handsome, he wondered why he had shown so little interest in girls.

"Thanks, Dad. We've even set a date." George hesitated.

"Good, good, we need to let the minister know. When?" Martha could hardly contain her excitement.

"Well, June 5 and no need to contact Rev. Raliegh. We're going to be married at Mount Holly."

"Oh. Of course, Susan's family makes that decision, that's right. I remember when Tom got married Gloria's family wanted the ceremony in the Methodist Church in Otsego." Martha began reconciling to the idea. She remained certain that Susan would leave her church and raise the children in the Methodist tradition set by the previous generations.

"We're getting married in a mass," George seemed uncomfortable.

Beverly watched as her brother turned red starting at the collar of his shirt. She wondered if she could be in the wedding. Tom and Gloria said she wasn't the right age to be anything in theirs, so she had always hoped she'd be the right age for one of the other brothers.

"That's just fine, George. Just ask what we're supposed to do about all the ritualistic stuff they do." Martha remained ignorant of any religion but her own.

"Listen, Mom and Dad, the Catholic Church won't marry us in the church with a full mass unless I convert to Catholicism." There he finally said it. "Did you hear me? I am converting to Catholicism."

At eleven years old, the words "I am converting to Catholicism," had little meaning to Beverly who was listening to the conversation between mouthfuls of roast beef and mashed potatoes. However, her mother's anguished cry, as if she had been shot, would always remain in Beverly's memory.

Her mother's continual asking, "Why are you doing this to me?" further puzzled Beverly who understood little of what this actually meant to her parents, but it didn't appear that George was doing much of anything to them.

"Mom, please understand. I've been studying the religion. It's giving me something that the Methodist doctrine never did. Please try to understand that it makes me happy."

"How dare you insult our religion that way! Susan's done this to you. I'll never forgive her!" Martha left the table in tears.

"George, how could you? You don't know what you're talking about. One girl comes along, and you throw away all that you've been raised to believe," Hollis said sadly.

Beverly would always remember the feeling of death that surrounded the house for weeks; weeks in which no one was allowed to speak about the announcement, weeks in which Susan was scarce near the house and George almost as scarce, weeks in which Martha's nostrils must have ached from the flaring, and weeks in which she spoke to no one, not even her other children.

However, like the Presbyterian wing, once the Canons realized they had lost and might even lose their son over this defection, they relented and the black cloud lifted, and the news was broken to the rest of the family. This in itself was a relief because now the parents found sympathy in the looks and nostrils of the other relatives.

Everyone came together for the wedding, and the Canons attended their first mass with no lightning bolts, and rumors of liquor and kegs of beer being brought out after Beverly and her family departed remained a quiet secret which no one discussed.

No one except the inner circle of Canons is aware that hard feelings are still held by Martha Canon. Even though Susan and George made a good marriage and had two sons, there are still times when they do not live up to the expectations of Martha. However, true to her form, she does not blame her own child. At those times, the family members hear her remark, "Well, you know, Susan is Catholic."

Beverly said good–bye to Laura and walked home in thoughtful silence remembering that day long ago when George had broken with tradition. How would her parents react if she brought

James Kelly home for dinner, she wondered. She decided not to think about it right now. She knew her parents would accept any friend of hers eventually. And besides, she was fairly certain that James wasn't Catholic.

CHAPTER FOUR

The opening game of the 1970–71 basketball season offered no excitement for the fans except for the fact that Victoria won easily, and James scored 24 points and made 16 rebounds, also easily. Already the town buzzed with talk of a state championship.

Beverly enjoyed watching James' graceful form run down the court. She held her breath every time he shot from the free throw line although there was no need. James made every shot. Once as he came off the court he even glanced at her in the bleachers and gave a slight wave. His muscles glistened in the harsh gym lights exposing his drenched and well–toned body to every eye in the place. None of those eyes watched him as eagerly as Beverly.

Beverly also saw Karen sitting two rows behind Coach Hoover. During half time she stopped for a visit on the way to the concession stand.

"Hi, Karen. Who'd ya come with?" Beverly asked.

"Uh, no one. I've heard so much about James from Coach that I had to come to see for myself. He's pretty good, don't ya think?"

"Pretty good? I'll say. Are you going to the dance?"

"Nah, I gotta get up and work at the store early tomorrow. Your dad said he had a funeral so that means I work all day." Karen's attention wandered as Coach Hoover came out of the locker room toward the scoring table. Her eyes followed him as he spoke to the record keeper. When he finished he looked up for a second and gave Karen a nod.

"You and Coach getting along all right this year?" Beverly asked softly.

"Yeah, just fine. He's really wonderful, you know," Karen whispered wistfully.

"How's his wife?"

"Fine, fine. I can't believe she doesn't come to see all of his games, though. If I was married to him, I'd be at every one," she said smugly missing Beverly's point entirely.

"Maybe it's too much for her. Listen, Karen, I gotta go. Take care of yourself, OK? And be careful," Beverly added as an after-thought.

"Sure, bye, Bev." Karen forgot about her quickly and didn't even hear the warning tone in her voice. Bill Hoover was climbing the bleachers to speak to her for a moment.

Later at the dance, James asked Beverly to dance to the first slow song. At first it seemed rather awkward with Beverly's small frame trying to reach up to James. He looked as awkward as she when he tried to bend his body at the knees to accommodate her.

He finally took her right hand, and they danced the way couples a decade before danced. They also laughed about it. Because they weren't holding one another close and seemed to be laughing more than not, no one really gave them any notice after the first few moments. When a fast song came on they decided to sit in the bleachers of the gym. James enjoyed watching Beverly hold down the back of her mini–dress in olive green as she climbed several steps up. She sat quickly and put her thin, shapely legs on the bench in front of her sweeping her long blonde hair onto her back away from her face.

"The Canon family, huh? You guys must own the whole town or something," James said teasing her.

"Just the north side of Main Street," she joked. "And don't forget, I'm also a part of the Stuart family."

"Really? Geez, you guys came over on the Mayflower or something, I bet," he said a little more seriously.

Beverly didn't think about her family much, but when James put it that way, she realized that they did have a long history especially in Victoria when Beverly's great–grandfather, Burton Canon opened the town's first funeral home almost 100 years ago on East Main three blocks from the downtown area.

Burton had loved all of the ritual associated with the mourning process and decided to study the science of embalming before opening his own funeral home where he could take care of the body before the actual mourning began. Then he could assist the families in practicing the correct rituals associated with helping the deceased enter into the other side.

As a side benefit and definite boost to his business, Burton's father, a furniture maker who had previously worked out of his home making custom pieces from dining room tables to coffins, saw a window of opportunity for his son and himself as he opened up the Canon Furniture Store also on Main Street, downtown across from the village square and town hall. In 1880, a dynasty was born.

When someone in Victoria died, Burton would send a messenger down to the furniture store and have his father begin work on the coffin. After a few years, with business booming, Burton Canon, Sr. began making coffins of varying degrees with fine woods and craftsmanship and built up a stock of coffins in different price ranges from which mourning families could choose. As the furniture store grew, so did the funeral home.

The upper floors of the Canon Funeral Home, which kept its dead and their mourners on the ground floor, had originally been the living quarters for the extended Canon family. However, as business grew in the 1890s, the family built a house behind the funeral home and turned the upstairs into a showcase for the finest coffins ever built in this area.

There were five rooms on the upper floor, and each room contained a minimum of five coffins. The first room contained the finest woods like mahogany. The softest satins in deep rich colors lined the inside of these final resting boxes.

Everyone entering the second floor to select a coffin walked by this room. Each room down the long hallway contained coffins, but in the last room the pine boxes sat alone with no fancy materials adorning their insides.

Burton would show the family members the coffins they said they could afford to buy, but then after they selected a simple pine box with no lining, he would lead them into the first room.

26

"Some families like to just look at what is available. These coffins are made out of the finest woods and certainly offer a peaceful resting place for a loved one," he would softly tell them.

Many times the grieving family began weeping and suddenly changed their minds deciding that going into debt a little more for the dear departed would be the only right thing to do.

Burton and his wife had two sons and a daughter. One son, George, became a Methodist minister and took up residency with his family at the parsonage across the street from his church. It was here that Hollis Canon, Beverly's father, was born in 1921.

Burton's other son, Paul took over his father's love of the dead and studied to become a mortician. No one had the skills of the elder Canon in crafting the coffins, but the furniture business was becoming so lucrative with the new Victorian style all the vogue in this area, that after the patriarch died in 1890 the furniture store became a retail store only. The workroom became an office for Paul who began running both the furniture and funeral businesses.

Paul and his wife never had any children so one of George's children would have to take over the financially successful business. Hollis as the eldest had the task dropped in his lap.

While Hollis had enjoyed hanging around the furniture store and smelling the oak, pine, and walnut woods entering and leaving the store, he never grew accustomed to the accouterments of the dead. But his father and uncle insisted that he learn both ends of the business, and so he went off unhappily to his year's study to become a mortician.

He hated every minute of his schooling and came home quite often until the United States entered World War II. He joined the service overnight without consulting his family.

While in school he picked up a secret and nasty habit. Whenever it came time to embalm a body, he embalmed himself as well to brace himself for the task ahead. No one knew his secret for many years. But a secret like this one doesn't keep forever as it begins to seep its way to the surface. It cannot be buried like the dead, but it can be ignored.

Beverly related some of this family history to James although she left out the part about her father's drinking and just told him the highlights.

"I'll save the part about my Aunt May for another time," Beverly said teasingly.

"Thanks, I don't think I could take much more of this success story. But how do the Stuarts fit in?"

"My mother, May Randall, and Connie Sammons are sisters with the maiden name of Stuart," she informed him.

"Connie Sammons, Mrs. Sammons the home ec teacher? And then, Joe Stuart, on the school board. . ."

"My uncle," Beverly admitted.

"Randall, as in Randall Ford?" James asked slightly in awe.

"Yeah, my Uncle Johnny owns the car dealership."

James whistled low between pursed lips. "Girl, you got a pedigree," he said almost sarcastically.

Beverly ignored his tone. She didn't think any of it was a big deal. Besides she couldn't stand May's husband, Johnny, who she had never seen sober. She loved Aunt May, but knew she suffered from a terrible marriage. She had no intention of telling James about that and her aunt's affairs. No one really talked about it much, but she had overheard enough conversations between her aunts to know that Aunt May also had her secrets.

"Hey, Bev, what's this about your Aunt May?" James seemed interested.

"I'll tell you some other time; it's no big deal, but she and my dad almost got married."

James looked at her incredulously. "I've got a feeling that's a pretty big story," he said as he pulled her to her feet to dance one more time to *Knights in White Satin.*

CHAPTER FIVE

When James went home after the dance, he thought about Beverly before he fell asleep. He liked the way she looked with her long blonde hair, bright blue eyes, and wide smile which always seemed welcoming to him. But he didn't quite trust her family. How could he? They had roots in Victoria and had probably been instrumental in keeping blacks out of the town for the past 100 years. Yet Beverly still attracted him, making him feel not quite so all alone in the cold winter of Victoria's welcome for newcomers.

The previous year, once the basketball season ended at VHS, James felt as if he was on vacation. No more late night practice and then the long hitch home. If he had extra money for gas, he could sometimes talk a teammate into giving him a ride the fifteen miles to his house; otherwise he had to hitch a ride standing on the outskirts of town on the highway heading to nowhere but a few farms and Ravens Wood Lake. It was not always an easy prospect to find a ride.

When getting home after dark was no longer a problem in the spring, he had a wider range of friends. Many of the farm boys tolerated James and sometimes even offered him rides and invitations to some of the spring and summer's best grassers. The invention of grassers came from these boys who created ways to fight the boredom of country living. One of the distractions centered around drinking and then finding a wide open grassy field on federal property on one of the local recreational lands or around one of the many private lakes in the area. Many times the boys had managed to buy a keg of beer but mostly those attending just brought a six pack of their own.

This group found many ways to entertain themselves that spring. Drinking beer went with everything. Painting on signs or better yet, stealing signs, also became a part of the ritual. And in between all this activity, they managed to squeeze in an increasingly

29

Patricia C. Behnke

more important activity—getting laid.

James was not wholly unfamiliar with the opposite sex. Since he turned twelve, older friends of his sisters had been coming on to him sexually in various ways. Many just tried to catch a glimpse of him undressing; and many of them wanted a little closer contact with him when they saw him without clothes on his body.

He had experimented with the bolder of the older girls and had even managed to go all the way once on the couch of his sister's apartment with her roommate one Sunday morning when his sister had gone out for doughnuts. For James, the feeling was beyond any imaginings in his narrow experience, and the actual act was quicker than he had thought it would be, but he was sure the next time would be different.

However, he felt something nearing exhilaration when he thought about the fact that his sister could have walked in at any moment, and for some musty, unspoken reason, this subterfuge enhanced the whole momentary affair; the first girl even became extraordinary in his mind; at least until he found another willing partner, and he began to think that most girls were the same to a certain degree.

He had not yet felt any particularly special feeling about any of his sexual partners. The field of girls became suddenly narrower because it depended on his sister's hospitality and her friends or roommates who made themselves available.

In Victoria and at home there had been few opportunities. However, one thing became apparent to James. From now on he would crave the feeling caused by sexual escapades that came from the uncertainty of being caught at any moment. Otherwise, he had little interest.

James's new found group of friends in Victoria understood that there seemed to be no girls around for James to "go out with." James wasn't sure how any one of them would feel about James dating his sister. The subject was not brought up until one very late night after cases of beer had been consumed under a star–lit sky.

Danny slurringly asked James, "Have ya got any lately?"

30

James decided his tone was friendly and responded, "There ain't much around here for me to get."

"Well, you just haven't been lookin' in the right places, man!" Danny slapped James on the back.

"That's right. You need to go to Dansville with us one night, James," another one of the guys offered.

"What's in Dansville but a pile of cow dung?" They all laughed.

"Just some of the best stuff you'll get around here." The others began poking and prodding each other.

"You mean pot?" James was puzzled.

"No, man, but it starts with "p" just the same!"

"Listen, James, there's some girls over there that only stay around for the spring and summer. They're from the migrant families. So you buy them some cigarettes, some beer, some candy, whatever. Then they give you whatever," Danny explained.

"You don't even have to be nice to 'em." Joey laughed until beer ran out his nose.

"When do we go?" James asked seriously.

So the boys all piled into Danny's pickup truck and drove down M–36 toward Dansville drinking beer and throwing cans at the signs as they hooted and hollered through the still cool Michigan spring night.

They stopped in the middle of a field. The headlights on the truck detailed a group of small run–down houses all in a row. Several girls standing near a campfire ventured over to the truck.

"Hey, what's up, sweetheart," Danny called to no one girl in particular.

"Nice truck. What you have for us tonight, Danny?" The tallest girl looked in the front seat. The others began to surround the back of the truck.

"Any beer?" one of them asked.

"Sure, baby, come and get it," Joey told her.

"Hey, how 'bout you, Mr. Tall and Dark?" The tiniest of the girls looked straight at James and pulled his face close to hers to give

31

him a long kiss. -

"How about you and me taking a walk, sweet thang," James said when they pulled apart.

The two walked into the woods and immediately set to work on each other. James didn't bother taking off her clothes except to pull her panties down. He didn't care much about anything except entering her and enjoying himself.

She cried out in pain at his sudden movement as he entered her without warning or little foreplay. He ignored her as he pounded over and over again at her tiny frame. He only stopped when he had spent himself.

"You bastard!" she screamed when he rolled off of her.

"What's wrong? You know you enjoyed it, too. You should be damn lucky I picked you." James zipped his pants and walked back to the pickup where everyone else seemed to be finishing up, too.

The whole thing left James empty. He felt more disgusted than satisfied. The girl he had been with hadn't even smelled good, and then she had the nerve to complain about him when she was nothing but a whore, he thought in disgust.

When the girl came running of the woods, the boys hooted and hollered. She kept screaming at Danny, "Never bring that bastard out here again. I'm hurt."

James joined in with the joking and teasing of the disheveled girl. He even threw a dollar bill on the ground at her feet. She spit on it and kicked it away from her.

"And that, my friends, is what my other friend Thomas Wang, Jr. can do for any young girl," James announced to his new buddies as they drove off into the dark night.

A better solution was offered when a local couple accepted a foreign exchange student from Brazil for the summer of 1970. Christina arrived toward the end of the school year and attended school with the family's children for the remainder of the semester. During the summer she would take courses at the University of Michigan in Ann Arbor, thirty–five miles away, in the same city where James' sister lived.

She was several years older than James and nearly as tall. Her exotic good looks and deep tan set off an intense explosion of sensuality for James. He poured on all of his sixteen year old charm. He teased and flirted and told her she looked like an Amazon.

"Are you sure you're not an Indian?" he would invitingly say.

Similarly, James excited Christina; he was like no one she had ever met, and besides none of the other local boys were wasting their time on her. She didn't fit the mold of Victoria and the locals ignored her because she was far too different, and therefore, unacceptable. Perhaps it was her accent, her height, or her brains, but so far no one but James had bothered to even talk to her. She had some experience with men and was eager to sample what America had to offer. She also had a curiosity about the vehemently denied bourgeois attitude regarding the races still in existence in the land of the free, brave, and equal.

Her foster parents for the summer provided little obstacle for the strong–willed Christina, although they did try to object.

Christina told them simply, "Call my parents. They will wonder why you bothered calling in the first place, since in my country we do not have the problem between the races as you do in this country."

This retort had the effect of shutting up the foster parents. They didn't want Christina's parents to think they couldn't handle their responsibility, or worse, to think the United States was a land riddled still with the issue of race. They finally agreed to let her date him on the weekends, so seeing him would not interfere with her studies.

And so began the summer of 1970 for James. Every morning that Christina had classes in Ann Arbor, she would drive by James' house first and take him with her. He would stay at his sister's who worked all day. Between classes she would slip over to the apartment where the two of them would spend hours exploring and learning about the intimacies of each other. It might be said that it became another class for Christina and one for James, as well, in the University of Life.

The satisfactory arrangement held benefits for both of them. James was happy because he was enjoying himself with no commitment. He knew she would only be here for a few more weeks; and Christina was happy for the same reason. They used each other; each knew it about the other one, and that made it even more memorable. It would be one of the last such relationships for both of them.

After a bittersweet good–bye for James and Christina, the summer of '70 ended, as she flew back home with memories to last her a lifetime during children, marriages, and just plain life; but always she would remember James and those sweet moments between classes. Her future degree would never show what she really learned that summer.

James began his junior year of high school confident as a man and as an athlete. He was sure this year would be the best yet.

And as he lay on his bed waiting for sleep to overcome his aching body tired from his first game of the season, he imagined how well things could go with Beverly as his girlfriend. His loneliness would be over and maybe, just maybe, with Beverly Canon by his side, he would be accepted by the townspeople who cheered him on to victory from the stands.

CHAPTER SIX

Beverly thought about James too before she fell asleep that night. She imagined having him hold her close as she told him her deepest secrets. She wondered if she would be able to trust him. So far she had learned when she did put her faith in something or someone, disappointment often followed. In those times she withdrew deep into herself and kept everyone at a distance. Often she became even cruel with those around her trying to make them feel as inadequate as she felt.

By the time Beverly met James in her sophomore year, she had discovered many things about boys. Even though she was raised in a family with mostly males, she knew little about them physically and emotionally. She just knew that very few of them were trustworthy. Even her brothers would tell on her if it suited their needs of the moment.

Two years earlier she had developed a crush on an upper classman. News about Beverly, pretty, popular and in a visible family, tended to be quite interesting to everyone in her school. Beverly, naively unaware of how gossip carried, multiplied the hurt by making the mistake of telling a few girlfriends about her liking Jack, and they, in turn, told older brothers, sisters, boyfriends, girlfriends, and anyone else who would listen.

It wasn't unusual for Jack to walk into the locker room at school and hear the taunts of his friends.

"Hey, Jack, hear you're taking out some jail bait. Cute little thing, that one," they'd tease as he came in from baseball practice.

"Lay off; she's too flat–chested for me." Jack's response would be met with hoots and hollers which soon left the locker room rolled down the hallways at school.

The worst morning came when Beverly walked past Jack's locker. He wouldn't turn to look at her but was ripping something out of his locker.

His buddies began cat calling and chanting, "Beverly loves Jack" as soon as she came into view.

"Aw, shut up, will ya," Jack yelled as he slammed his locker shut.

Soon she learned the reason. Someone had broken into Jack's locker and on a red construction paper heart, had placed both Jack's and Beverly's school photo with love messages written across it. Jack assumed wrongly that it was Beverly's handiwork, and Beverly, with sinking heart, realized it had to have been one of her "closer friends" because she had only given out a few photos that school year.

One day in study hall someone who had been signing Beverly's yearbook, passed it on to Jack for his autograph.

"To a sweet kid, but since you're so young, you might as well forget it," he scrawled before passing it back.

Laura found Beverly crying in the bathroom later that day and finally she pried the news from Beverly.

"You got a lotta nerve, Jack! Why can't you be a little nicer?" Laura yelled at Jack when she saw him walking out of school that afternoon.

"What ya mean?"

"I mean, why did you have to go and ruin Beverly's yearbook like that?"

"I didn't ruin it. Besides she's ruining my year. Tell her to leave me alone," he said as he briskly strode past Beverly's loyal friend.

"Don't worry, you bastard, I'll tell her." Laura walked away before he could respond.

The boys seemed particularly cruel, and she didn't understand that their teasing about her lack of breasts and her crushes were the only way the boys felt comfortable around her. She didn't realize they wanted her attention, which she refused to give to anyone involved in the Jack fiasco. She also didn't realize that they would do or say anything for attention, even if it made her cry or shout in anger. Beverly's sensitivity made her believe that everyone was as honest as she was about feelings. However, she did not know that many people hid their feelings behind shows of bravado. Most people were just not as brave as Beverly had been. It's probable the boys never realized their attraction to her; certainly Beverly didn't see it as attraction. She thought they all hated her, seeing it as one more rejection. Her life in and out of school filled itself with all types of rejections in those days.

One of the Canon boys, Dave, had just been arrested for selling marijuana in Ann Arbor while attending the University of Michigan. This scandal brought shame and unbelievable heartache on Hollis and Martha Canon. He had acted alone, and there were no Catholics or Baptists to blame for his illegal dalliances.

Although Beverly cried for her brother, she also cried for herself, and the lack of attention given to her life. She hated coming into that house of gloom which contained various sets of relatives on any given night during the period of arrest, arraignment, trial, and sentencing. She ached for the attention needed from her parents during her crucial adolescence which was proving to be more difficult than most. The house had taken on features of the funeral home with no funeral or wake in sight, just the nightly mourning and remembering and trying to put responsibility on someone. Nostril flaring was at a premium.

Martha Stuart Canon, in particular, wanted to find someone to blame because she had been humiliated in front of her entire family. With her short stature, large nose, and wiry dark hair, she had never received the kind of attention and regard that everyone seemed to give so easily to her sisters, Connie and May.

Martha came from a family as equally prominent as the Canons in town except not as wealthy. Her father, Reverend Edward Stuart, took over the pulpit from George Canon upon his untimely death in 1936 after preaching one Sunday morning. George just went home and quietly sat in his easy chair in the living room of the parsonage and had a simple, massive heart attack. His wife took solace in the fact that his brother, Paul, would make him look less dead and more natural at the Canon Funeral Home.

The Stuart family had three daughters and two sons. They filled the parsonage to the brim when they moved into the rambling house across the street from the Methodist Church. The Canon and Stuart families had many interactions during the transition period as Mrs. Canon found a place to live for herself and her two almost grown sons. For the time being, they would live with Paul and his childless wife who were planning to retire in three years after Hollis went to school and came back for his apprenticeship for one year with his uncle.

Martha was still in the primary grades when the family moved to Victoria, but her sister May was one year behind Hollis at the high school. Since there were only about twenty students in each class much mingling took place between all levels with the upper classmen. Also May and Hollis had their church activities in common and became quite close very quickly.

May embodied all the beautiful features of the Stuart family. Her sandy brown hair waved around her face framing a small nose and perfectly formed lips. Hollis couldn't help but be entranced by her beauty. They began the time–honored tradition of dating under very supervised conditions and soon Hollis fell in love with May.

While Hollis fell in love with May, May fell in love with what Hollis could offer her. She couldn't wait to leave the crowded parsonage and have her own place and her own money to spend. Hollis would be able to provide her with that. She also liked his looks and knew they made a striking couple. Hollis, six feet tall, stood six inches above May. He kept his lanky frame in shape by playing tennis daily, spring through fall. May loved to see Hollis in his tennis whites with his muscular legs carrying the same blonde hair which covered his head. With his blue eyes and her hazel ones, she knew they would create beautiful children who would be the envy of Victoria. The perfect family with the perfect house, car and life.

However, when Hollis joined the service after the bombing of Pearl Harbor in late 1941, the relationship ended. In the spring of

1942, May married Johnny Randall. Hollis didn't return to Victoria until 1945.

By this time, Martha had grown up and had just turned sixteen. She just knew her sister had hurt Hollis horribly by marrying Johnny. Martha had developed a crush on Hollis ever since he had first started dating May. He had always been sweet to Martha, not like that Johnny Randall who was now her brother–in–law. The only good thing she could see from that relationship was her little nephew, JJ, born seven months after the marriage.

Martha babysat for her nephew many nights while May and Johnny went out drinking. She also came over and cared for him on those nights when May hosted her big parties which always ended up with someone trading punches. And she knew Johnny kept up his old ways because she had caught him with other women in various parts of the house during those parties. May never seemed to notice.

Martha also noticed that Hollis Canon never went anywhere in public except maybe to church occasionally with his mother after his return from the war. And then he barely spoke to her. She decided to write him a note boldly inviting him over to visit with her sometime.

At first Hollis wasn't sure who the Martha of the short note could be. But then he remembered May's kid sister. He decided to check her out the next week at church. When she saw Hollis approach, she smiled shyly. He noticed right away that she wasn't beautiful like May, and she didn't exude the confidence and sexuality of May. He liked that and felt that she might be a safer choice than her sister. He asked her out that very day.

They were married in February of 1946. And their first child, Tom, wasn't born until a full year later. Several years later George was born. By 1950 Martha ached for a little girl and begged Hollis for another child.

When Dave was born, the doctor came into the recovery room where Martha lay coming out from under the anesthesia.

"Well, Martha, when he came out, I saw that little thing dangling there and I said to myself, 'Now Martha wants a little girl awfully bad,' so I slapped it first this way and then that but it still wouldn't come off. So I guess you've got your third boy."

Martha smiled at him dully and went into a severe depression for the next three years until she became pregnant again. When her only daughter was born, she quit begging Hollis to sleep with her.

After Dave's marijuana arrest, before the trial, Martha, Hollis, and Dave attended therapy sessions; mainly because it would look good to any judge who might take notice. It certainly went against the Canon creed of strength and solving one's own problems by ignoring them. However, the time had come to assign guilt.

Beverly asked her mother how the session had gone that day.

"Very well! Dave finally told us why he's been so resentful all these years, and we're going to work on that," Martha announced almost gleefully.

"What is it?" Beverly asked.

"Well, Beverly, evidently your brother's troubles all started with your birth when Dave was four. He felt abandoned because we turned all of our attention to you. What a relief! I really thought I had done something that had caused all of this trouble." Martha smiled in relief.

Beverly at fourteen, felt as if a noose had been slipped around her neck. Her mother could sigh with much satisfied relief, because now she no longer had to take full responsibility. However, Martha Canon had no idea what she had done to her daughter.

In that instant of confession, Beverly hated her mother and turned from her once and for all. No more confiding would ever take place between mother and daughter, confiding that was desperately needed in Beverly's life at this time. Beverly's parents were unaware of her so they didn't notice. They did not ask about her life anymore, nor were they involved in any of the events that make up the life of a fourteen year old. They simply had no time for her; all their energy went to the third son who would never have gotten into trouble if not for THE BIRTH OF BEVERLY.

Unaware of anything but their own misery, they did not

realize that what they had done to their son when Beverly was born, was exactly what they were doing to Beverly now to atone themselves.

In addition to the broken trust, Beverly now had to deal with the guilt of being born at all. She was effectively cut off from her family of which she no longer felt a part.

In fact, in one swift moment Beverly realized that she had no one but herself to depend on and at fourteen she became independent, rebellious, disrespectful of authority, and she learned the art of showing off her intelligence, body, and cruel wit. Beverly became an imitator of people. The harsher and more exaggerated the imitation, the more laughs she received from her peers. She was popular, at other's expense, but didn't feel close to anyone, except Laura.

She had no use for the boys her own age, and she never really knew from the eighth grade on, who was a friend or who just wanted something else. Therefore, she insulated herself by pretending not to care, which made her more popular. Actually underneath she was in pain and cried herself to sleep many nights.

Into this life waltzed the perfect solution: James Kelly. James became in her mind everything the other boys were not. He treated her with more respect and when with him, she knew he liked her. Unaware of the games played by the white boys in Beverly's circle, James always remained straightforward with her. He had no reason not to because he not yet known rejection. Beverly also enjoyed the fact that he was talented and very nearly famous.

However in the off season, James did not receive the same adulation heaped on him during the basketball season. The tolerance of his presence weakened when spring, summer and fall rolled around. Accordingly, some of the older locals became a little concerned about rumors: James dating Christina during the summer, and partying with the farmers' sons. Many felt these situations should be watched and had loudly informed Bill Hoover, the basketball coach, of their concerns.

They left him with the responsibility to see that nothing happened. The coach's job is only as secure as his standing in the

Patricia C. Behnke

community. The parents in Victoria acted as back seat drivers to their athletic coaches, and they didn't like detours or road obstructions in their town.

Beverly was on the verge of discovering her own sexuality although she couldn't have said as much. She knew that on vacations away from Victoria she attracted boys, and she liked being kissed and held. This past summer she went away with a neighbor family and had two boys fighting over her.

So, as the basketball season for James' junior year began and with Beverly's sophomore year just barely underway, both of the teenagers thought about the other and wondered what would happen next. They both knew something more would happen between them. The consequences never entered the minds of these adolescents, and if they had realized it, perhaps the attraction would have been even stronger and would have drawn them closer together sooner.

Beverly pondered Laura's cautious words from several days before and wondered if what she said could possibly be true. Her parents, devout Methodists, had always taught her that all people were created equal. She had no idea that her parents' true beliefs had nothing whatsoever to do with what they preached.

CHAPTER SEVEN

"We're number one, we're number one!" The shouts echoed
everywhere Beverly went that winter. The basketball team had lost
no games by Christmas. VHS was hosting the Christmas tournament,
and it remained on the Victorian mind that they would finally show
all the neighboring towns invited to their gymnasium their new
improved team by sweeping the entire tournament. Even those
schools much larger than Victoria were invited, and the tournament
wins were often balanced unfairly toward the larger high schools.
Not this year, not with James Kelly starting as VHS's center.

Described by papers in Detroit as "one of the finest sharp-
shooters in the state," the 6–foot–8, James averaged 25 points and 26
rebounds per game by the time of the Christmas tournament. In one
game against neighboring Fowlerville, James had scored 47 points.

"Can you come to a party with me after Friday's game?"
James casually asked one day as he leaned on Beverly's locker.

Beverly's heart pounded so hard she thought it would burst
through her soft pink sweater before she could answer that she would
try except for one small problem. "My parents don't allow me to date
yet," she explained.

"How about if you come to the party with your friends, then,
and we'll meet up there?" James thought quickly.

That seemed the easiest solution since Beverly had planned
on going to the kegger at Tommy's house anyway. The whole school
would be there. Tommy's parents were in Hawaii, and he lived in
the country. A perfect arrangement for teenagers in a small town.
Beverly would soon be sixteen, the magic age of a teenager. A
license to drive and date all in one birthday.

Beverly had not confided in any of her friends yet about her
feelings for James. Maybe that wasn't so surprising given Laura's
initial reaction. Also, Beverly didn't know if she was ready to admit

her feelings for James. Besides, she told herself, there was really nothing to tell. So far, they had only innocently flirted and danced a few times.

The team easily beat Hamburg that Friday night, 78–52. James alone scored 32 points. Near Christmas, the night was cold and the sky held bright twinkling lights against its ink black darkness, and the air held the promise of snow. As footsteps crunched on the frost–covered sidewalk and nostril hairs froze together, everyone looked forward to this party at one of the rambling farm houses on the outskirts of town.

Beverly had acquired a new habit in her most troubled year. She liked to drink with her friends whenever possible. That in itself was not shocking in this small town. Drugs had slowly been seeping into this small community mostly in the form of marijuana. However, the main form of entertainment still centered around drinking.

Beverly's drinking became a problem sometimes. When she drank she became funnier, and her imitations so much crueler; this also made her drink more. Many weekend nights she came crawling into her parents' house a boozy, vomity mess. No one noticed at her house. No one ever said a word to her as long as they heard the door open and close by midnight, and Beverly's common sense brought her home by midnight every Friday and Saturday.

On the night of this party, nervousness about being alone with James for the first time, caused her to drink even more than usual. She wore her drunkenness in her walk and talk when she entered the party.

James too had had his share of alcohol by the time he arrived. However, he drank in celebration not from nervousness. But when he saw Beverly enter he knew she was feeling even finer than him. She came over immediately and sat on his lap which at first startled James because they had not so much as touched in their innocent flirtations together. James had not seen this side of her. He didn't object; he just found himself temporarily stunned.

"Hey, baby, you were wonderful tonight," Beverly breathed close to his ear.

44

"I tried, Bev, I tried." James laughed from pleasure in feeling her small body curled up in his lap with her head now nestled in his neck.

"James," Beverly hesitated.

"Yeah, sweet thang?"

"How come you never kissed me?"

James immediately pulled her chin so their lips met. He gave her a long lingering kiss tentatively exploring with his tongue for a short moment.

"Whatcha mean I never kissed ya?" James said as he began to rub her back.

They became engrossed in each other, nibbling and tentatively giving more kisses. Even though they sat in a corner of the living room, and the room contained only the dimmest of lights, they had become the focal point of the party. Light against dark stood out against the blue–flowered pattern of the rocking chair they occupied.

The exploration never went any further that first night, however. Beverly's friends began pulling her away with shouts that they had to go. They still had a curfew even if Beverly had forgotten. Their pleas carried a different kind of desperation although Beverly seemed unaware of it. They sensed trouble. No one had suspected before this night that there might be something more than friendship between the two of them.

By the next morning the gossip had started. At this point no one told parents. A conspiracy had developed to keep it from the parents. It might affect all of them if word got out. The other teenagers seemed to understand, if Beverly and James did not, that the news of their togetherness would rock the foundations of their parents' lives and might result in the imposition of restrictions on all of them.

However, the news did reach Coach Hoover. Not much older than the students and just five years out of college, Hoover became privy to all sorts of information that other adults weren't. He maintained an easy camaraderie with his players that resulted in their trust. As he came into the locker room Monday morning he overheard a few of them talking.

"What'd ya think about Bev and James Friday night?" one of the boys asked to no one in particular.

"I can't believe her. She's wild, but James Kelly? Come on."

"Yeah, I know it. I thought about asking her out once, but not now," another one said.

"What are you boys talking about?" Coach Hoover interjected.

"Coach, your star had some fun Friday night after the game." Donny and the others began slapping each other on the back and laughing.

"Oh yeah? What happened?"

"Well, James was just sitting there minding his own business when Bev Canon came stumbling in all drunk and stuff. She went and sat right in his lap and then they started making out until her friends pulled her away. It was something," Donny pronounced.

"I'll bet it was. Where's James now? Which class?"

"Gee, I don't know, Coach."

"That's all right. I'll get Karen to find him," he said as he walked back to his office.

Only a few of the students realized Bill Hoover had a penchant for the young beautiful girls who passed through the halls of VHS. Each year he chose one senior girl to be his office aide before, during, and after school. Sometimes only those students close to the particular girl involved ever suspected that he was more than just good old Coach Hoover to those few females who received his special attention. But like Hollis Canon's drinking, some secrets have a way of seeping up to the surface.

This year he had chosen Karen Adams who came from one of the poorer families in town. Her parents worked long hours in a factory in Dexter which made easy access to her. Karen also worked some afternoons and weekends at the Canon Furniture Store.

This gossip about James and Beverly scared the Coach; it involved his star player, his ride to the pinnacle of his coaching career. Moreover Beverly's aunts, uncles, and cousins were colleagues of his. One uncle even held a school board position. The interracial situation made it explosive, and he could not afford to have his star discovery, James Kelly, involved in any scandal that might jeopardize the teams' chances at the state championship game in March. Besides he thought to himself that it just wasn't right. James should date girls of his own kind. That was only natural.

He rationalized that James could be influenced negatively if he continued seeing her since it was the Canon girl who was drunk, not James. Even if it wasn't for the explosiveness of this particular situation, drinking and sexual experimentation alone could prove fatal to James' ability on the court. He would have to do something quickly.

"Karen, look up James Kelly's schedule and send for him," Coach demanded as he walked back into his office.

"Sure thing, Coach." Karen smiled demurely and walked over to the schedule cards on the counter. She bent over slightly to reach a pad of paper on the lower shelf revealing long, firm thighs.

"Karen, don't do that, please," he groaned.

"What do you mean," Karen asked as she turned around with a wide grin on her face.

"You know what I mean. Not during school hours." He swiveled his chair around to the counter behind him to look for the plays for Friday's game.

When Karen came back with James, Coach Hoover asked her to go to the front office for awhile so he could be alone with James.

Coach looked at his star player. "This girl could influence you in the wrong way," he began.

"Aw, Coach, it was just a little hugging and kissing at a party. Nothing to worry about!"

"James, a wrong move at this time in your career could end it, and I'm concerned for your chances at a college career and someday, pro. Don't blow it now. There will be plenty of chances for girls in the off season and later."

"Coach, I think you're making too big a deal out of this. It

47

was just one party."

"Am I? James, I know this town, and I also understand the sexual signals a girl of sixteen can send out, especially one who looks like Beverly, but what kind of girl shows up at a party smashed?"

"A party girl?" James suggested, hoping this would lighten the coach's dark mood.

"Don't get funny with me! I'm just concerned about you. Why not consider dating one of the girls your age from Ravens Wood Lake?"

That question hung in the air for uncomfortable moments. James had trusted the coach up until then.

"I mean, for your sake, it would be easier. Dating Beverly will mean trouble for you, I guarantee it. I know the family well; I've known other families like the Canons. No matter how the rest of the town sees her, the Canons view her as a prized possession. They won't care that you are the star if you mess with her! Now, James I'm telling you this because I don't want to see you hurt."

"I understand, Coach. It would really hurt me if the team didn't win state, too." James winked to let the coach know nothing had escaped him.

Coach would have to watch what he said from here on, but he knew James would stay away from the girl for now. He just needed some extra insurance to seal the deal, he thought as he sent Karen to bring Beverly from study hall.

"What's he want, Karen?" Beverly asked as they walked back to the office together.

"I don't know, Bev, but James just left. Coach's acting a little weird, too, you know agitated."

Beverly said nothing but wondered if Karen might be the reason for his agitation. She didn't care about Coach, but she didn't want to see Karen get in trouble.

"Now, Beverly, I understand you had quite a time at the party Friday night," Coach said as Beverly settled herself in the chair still warm from James' heat.

Only the sharp jerk of her head indicated her surprise that he had this information. At first Beverly had wondered if Coach might be sending for her to become his office aide. But Beverly didn't need to worry that he might put the moves on her. For one thing, he remained quite loyal throughout the year to the chosen one, and second, Beverly didn't possess the winning combination for the Coach's off–the–court appetite. She lacked the buxomy, sultry look he craved and which Karen had.

Coach Hoover continued to wait for an answer. She decided to play it cool, and let him get to the point. She wasn't about to help him out.

"I also know you had a good time with James at this party. I don't think I need to tell you what this situation could mean to you and to James. First of all, I know your parents, and I know they disapprove strongly of alcohol. I definitely know what they would say about their only daughter drinking. They would also blame James; he's a convenient scapegoat. Your parents could destroy him. Where would we be then?"

"What do you want from me?" Beverly kept silent about her father and his disapproval of alcohol, but she knew he was right about her mother and finding scapegoats.

"Promise not to see James again, and I keep my mouth shut."

Since Coach had made a few good points about certain things, James and Beverly both agreed in part to his request even though neither one of them respected him. Not overly upset about the matter, they felt that they had just been given a great exciting gift. From now on all their encounters would be secret, silent, and sneaky.

CHAPTER EIGHT

The Christmas tournament held in Victoria, proved to be a great success. VHS came out the victor in all the games and came away with not only an immense trophy but also the respect of the neighboring towns. James played some of the best games of his career. And because titles and win/loss records were not affected by this non–district play, even the opposing teams cheered when he made a spectacular rebound or an impossible basket.

It was also successful for James and Beverly because the pretense of post–game gatherings gave them a chance to see each other. No one seemed to notice that they both came up missing at the same time. As long as they stayed away from the center of the party, no one paid much attention. That one drunken evening was nearly forgotten and only remembered as just a party happening, with nothing serious involved. Beverly and James didn't act any differently and rarely appeared in public together, and so no one thought much about them.

People see and believe what they want to believe because if they had looked hard enough, they would have noticed the closeness between the two of them. They would have noticed that James sought out Beverly in the stands before each game as he stood near his teammates on the floor. They would have noticed that the slight wave and nod he directed to the stands was reserved solely for Bev. And they would have noticed the smile and blush that appeared on Beverly's face as she acknowledged his private salute.

But so far James and Beverly only talked when alone. Sometimes they kissed and cuddled to keep warm in the cold Michigan December nights, but tons of clothes and Beverly's shy innocence kept these sessions from going much further.

Their bond grew from the fact that they had a secret which no one else knew. This secret made them cohorts in a game caused by others and created by themselves. It brought them closer together and even made them more determined to see one another.

"Bev, when do you turn sixteen?" James asked one night.

"January tenth, why?"

"Just wondering if you'll be dating then."

"Dating who?"

"Anyone. You told me once you couldn't date until you turned sixteen. I was just wondering. And you know what Coach said about us dating."

"James, how can you think I'd go out with someone else? And who cares about Coach? He's a jerk."

"Yeah, I know, but he can help me get what I want, you know."

"What do you want?"

"State championship. That's what I want just as much as him. That's why we can't date openly until after that."

"Why do you want it so much?"

"So I can get out of here and be someone and be respected. I want it so badly, I can taste it, baby. And you could come along with me, if you wanted," James said as he held her tenderly under the moonlit winter sky.

"I want it, too, James, I do. And March isn't that far away." Beverly reached up and pulled his face close to hers and kissed him softly.

"Ah, Bev, come on, baby, I can't stand it when you do that stuff," James groaned.

"Why not?" she asked softly caressing his cheek.

"'Cuz I know you won't let me do what I really want to do."

"James, I'm not ready, please understand."

"Come on, sure I understand. But don't be so sexy with me like that. You don't know what it does to me."

Their meetings mostly took place out of doors. Neither had a car, and they didn't trust anyone else enough to ask to borrow a one. Even though it was bitter cold that winter, they didn't notice. They hugged under black skies and held hands under moonlit ones. They could see their breath, and it was exciting to them to sit outside of a party, just the two of the them against the world.

Beverly had gained a friend she trusted. She could confide in James all the things she had previously shared only with Laura. Most importantly to Beverly, he understood. He cared and wanted to know everything about her. But best of all for Beverly, she was sure he wouldn't tell anyone else. Her secrets were safe and because she had bared her soul, she was sure she would never have cause to doubt him. She trusted him implicitly because absolutely no one in her life had ever formed such a strong bond with her.

He wasn't quite so sure of her. He knew she was the first white person he had ever felt comfortable with, and he even forgot his anger at the unfairness of the world when he was with her. When he sat alone in his darkened bedroom at night, he sometimes contemplated this phenomenon.

She, of all whites, should invoke the most hatred. Her ancestors had probably aided in enslaving his ancestors. Her family still wore the masks of superiority, and her people had helped to create the all–white enclave of Victoria.

When Coach had revealed himself over the Beverly issue, James knew for sure that most people still considered him in a separate category and that the only reason he was tolerated in this white village was because he brought fame and excitement to them. He knew if he stepped out of line, the charade would be over. He also knew in his bones that if anything criminal or suspicious occurred in this community, he would be the first suspect.

Yet, James felt none of these feelings when alone with Beverly. She exhibited no signs that she felt superior to him or that she felt as if he was separate from her. In fact, she seemed to value his opinion and confided deep, dark secrets and yearnings to him during their talks. He didn't have to prove himself to her. He didn't have to be best at anything. He was nearly certain that Beverly would consider him a friend even if he wasn't the star of the team.

For now he remained content to hold her hand, hug her and kiss her, and be a gentleman in her presence. However, he was still a young virile male who thought he needed and deserved more. He wouldn't scare Beverly off because in her he could see fragments of his future, but he still had needs.

He was almost seventeen and used to having sex often with various willing partners. Therefore, he rationalized, it would not hurt to have a sexual relationship with some of the girls around town. Since the season had started, he knew some girls who would have him anyway they could get him. He didn't see the harm in having them around while he kept Beverly as his important girl.

And so began a double espionage period for James. He sneaked to see Beverly, and after she left the parties, he would sneak away with one of the girls who were willing to give him what he wanted. He only wanted one thing from them. He knew that they couldn't provide him with the status and legitimacy that Beverly could because they didn't come from the same type of families. Most of them were poor and lived on the outskirts of town. Their families either worked in factories in nearby towns or hired themselves out to the local onion and sod farms during the summer season. He confided in his buddies about these girls so he could borrow a car for his purposes. Guys will keep secrets like this one.

Life became very exciting that winter in Victoria. The unusual sight of the journalists and newscasters from the larger surrounding cities at the basketball games became commonplace. As February of 1971 began drawing to a close, it became obvious to the townspeople that the team would most certainly make it to the state championship games. They had not lost a game yet. Long before the season ended, they wore the crown of undisputed champion of the district.

While James dominated the boards during most of the season's games, the starting guards formed an unbeatable duo with exceptional shooting and ballhandling. The combination on the courts had so far been untouchable and brought Coach Hoover's overall career record to 66–15 with 44 of those wins in the last 45 games.

All that lay ahead now were the regional, quarter–finals,

semi–finals, and then the state championship games in Crisler Arena in Ann Arbor.

A new tradition in pep rallies had begun in Victoria the previous year when the team made it to regionals. Even though they lost in the last round of regional play, the unique pep rally resurrected itself as the team headed off to regionals slightly more confident this year.

Instead of having the typical pep rally in the gym, the entire school took to the streets. The basketball team rode on the fire engine, and the band followed continuously playing the school's fight song. Then came the rest of the student body who were followed by the townspeople coming out of their houses and stores in the slush that is late February in Michigan. Around and around the village square they went screaming, "We're number one!" and "We love you, James!" Quite heady stuff for sixteen and seventeen year olds. Even though the other players weren't the stars, they certainly enjoyed the fame offered them by starting on the first winning team in Victoria in as long as they could all remember.

The other starters, especially Harry Thomas and Rick Lewis, were decent ball players and would have had a chance at the district title without James, but they certainly wouldn't have won as handily nor would the town be as optimistic about their chances for a state championship as they were now. All the sports writers agreed that James created the sensation because of his size, but with Harry and Rick there to loft high, arching passes toward the basket, James tipped in many a ball while running backwards much to the crowd's delight. Even the fans of the opposing teams cheered some of the top form action by James and his teammates.

When the fire engine stopped at the village square, the team climbed the steep stairs leading up to the imposing town hall. James searched the crowd for Beverly. Other girls who provided his sexual release while freezing his behind in the back seat of cars, now shouted for his attention; even others he had not experienced bounced in his direction. However, it didn't matter on this day; he wanted to share it with Beverly, and for the first time this year, she wasn't there.

In fact, Beverly had been all set to attend the pep rally until an encounter with Donna during the rush to leave school to become a part of the giant pep rally. Donna, who came from a farm family, detained Beverly. Beverly hid her surprise because she and Donna had very little in common and even though they had been in school together since they both were five, never socialized or ran with the same group of friends.

"I sure do understand now why you were with James at Tommy's party before Christmas. Isn't he the greatest? Have you ever thought about going out with him again? I mean, did he approach you for a date after that one time?"

Beverly stared at her dumbfounded unable to even shake her head.

"I'm wondering because after the party last weekend, he hasn't said one word to me, and I wondered why. I wouldn't mind being with him again, that's for sure," Donna continued unaware of Beverly's shock.

On and on Donna rambled about James. Luckily, she became lost in her own little telling of her adventure with the basketball star. She didn't notice the lack of color in Beverly's face or the lack of response from her mouth.

Beverly knew she would have to respond eventually, but she also knew Donna was fairly well self–absorbed on most occasions. Beverly wouldn't have to say much before she fought her way home. She felt a hole opening up beneath her feet, and if she didn't move soon, she would be swallowed by the gaping black abyss. She was finding it increasingly hard to breath.

"So, I said 'sure, I'd love to.' What do you think, Beverly, do I have a chance?"

"Probably just as good as anyone else, Donna. Good luck, and don't miss the pep rally. James likes his girls to be fans," she managed to choke out before turning and walking away.

Pain racked her body; she felt as if James had stabbed her and her life. She had trusted him with so much of herself and had felt so close to him. Yet he had left her Friday night and gone to someone else. Did he tell Donna the same things: that she was beautiful, that he had never known anyone like her, that he had never felt so comfortable with anyone else? Beverly simply couldn't bear it. He had lied to her. She had seen in James someone with whom she could join her life, and he had betrayed her just like all the rest of the people she had trusted before.

One thing James had done for her was to curtail her drinking. She hadn't been drunk once since Tommy's party several months earlier. She didn't need anything to become comfortable with James. She just was, and besides, James had voiced disapproval of "his girl" drinking, even though he still did.

What did it matter now? That's exactly what she wanted to do—get drunk. She decided she would go to the game after all that night, but not on the pep bus as planned. She knew a few friends who were driving to the game, and she decided to join them. After a quick call to Joey, she had a ride to the game and beer for the ride there. Guzzling beers and kissing one of her "boy friends" in the back seat, allowed Beverly to arrive at the game in a fairly disheveled shape.

When James saw her mid–way through the game, he was angry. He also felt betrayed because she knew how important this game was to him. They were facing the stiffest competition so far this season, and he needed her in his corner. She hadn't attended the pep rally, and now she shows up, obviously drunk. The smirk on her face and the far–off look in her eyes gave her away. She was also obviously with a date. James curtailed most of his anger during half time. He tried to forget about her mocking him with her sarcastic grimace in the stands while he played the best game of his career. He became determined not to let a girl get to him. It worked this one time, and VHS won the first game of regional play, 76–68 with James scoring 29 points and intimidating the defense of the opposing team.

When the players reached town, it seemed the whole of Victoria came out to greet and applaud them in the school's lobby. Only one more game, and they would be the regional champs and then on to the final rounds. However, when James disembarked from the bus, he searched the crowd frantically once again for Beverly, and she wasn't there.

Of course, there was a party afterwards. It seemed someone's parents were always conveniently out of town that winter so the parties could be held indoors and not out in a field somewhere as they were in the summer. James and Beverly had an unspoken agreement to always meet up at these parties, and he sure needed to talk to her tonight about her behavior, and once that was out of the way, about his excitement over the game.

When he arrived he didn't see her at first. A closer inspection found her on the lap of one of his farm buddies. She was guzzling a beer at the moment he spotted her. When she saw him, she leaned down and kissed Joey full on the mouth. James had never known such anger. He had never had an emotion overtake him so quickly. It gave him no time for rational thought. He raced to the clutching couple and pushed Beverly off of his lap. He pulled Joey up by the collar and punched him in the jaw with a powerful right hook. Joey never knew what had hit him before he hit the floor.

As soon as James had hit him, rational thought came back as quickly as the anger had swept over him. His anger at Beverly and Joey dissipated and now he felt disgust for himself because he had let a girl, a white girl, cause him to lose control. It was dangerous, and he vowed then it would be the last time. He suddenly realized that the whole room was frozen in time and staring at him. No one knew exactly what had happened, but light began dawning on the more sober ones.

Joey was completely taken by surprise as James helped him up off the floor. He heard James apologizing but didn't understand why or what had provoked James, his buddy, to slug him like that. He couldn't fathom that James was jealous. James could have any girl he wanted at the moment, and he usually did. Beverly wasn't going with anyone, Joey thought as he looked at James. James told him they would talk later, but for now he had to settle something else. He had to straighten Beverly out; Beverly, who had seemed the enemy moments earlier, suddenly appeared as a frightened child watching him carefully.

He grabbed her arm causing her to wince in pain, but he was not conscious of his strength. However, he did use it as a weapon now to show his power over her. They went outside as people made a pathway through the living room for them. The room was silent for only a moment after the front door slammed, and then it sounded like bees swarming around a lilac bush as the gossip swirled and several dove for the uncurtained windows.

CHAPTER NINE

"You're hurting my arm; let me go!" shrieked Beverly as they tumbled down the front steps of the house.

Beverly, not quite sober, couldn't understand. James acted angry, but wasn't she the one who was supposed to have all the anger? Hadn't he lied and cheated? Why was he treating her so roughly?

"You're going to listen to me now, baby. Who the hell do you think you are, drinking and making out in front of everybody in there? Why weren't you at the pep rally this afternoon? I don't allow anyone to treat me like that!"

"Who the hell do you think you are," screamed Beverly who by now was an unattractive mess, and her voice had taken on the dimension of a screeching bird. Through it all, however, she noted a change in James' tone. She was not aware enough to realize the change might indicate danger for her as she continued.

"Why aren't you in the back seat of some car screwing Donna?"

James' backhanded slap landed across Beverly's right cheek. Stunned, Beverly just stared up at him. It seemed unbelievable that her gentle James could hurt her in any way, but something had changed between them. They would never be able to go back to the easy conversations of before. Suddenly James was in charge, and he expected Beverly to fall in line.

"Are you calm enough to listen to me now? I'm not going to take this kind of crap anymore. You will not drink or be with other guys without me there. You will not scream and tell me what I should be doing, or the same thing will happen. Is that clear?"

Numbly Beverly nodded. Part of her wanted to run and rebel against this extreme form of authority, but she was rooted to the ground, immobile. Overcome by the change in him, she suddenly forgot his betrayal and her anger. She became the submissive child completely under the control of James simply because he said so.

"I'll be with other girls like Donna, as long as you refuse. When you decide the time is right, I'm here. I won't fight or beg for that because I don't need to. But until you decide that's what you want, I'll be with other girls whenever I want. Understand?"

Again she nodded numbly, although there was no need. He hadn't made a request; he had made a command. She would accept all of his conditions. She had always despised weak women, her mother included, and now she had joined their ranks without a thought. It didn't seem important to her now, though. What stood out in her mind was the amount of emotion James had displayed with her. No one had ever shown extreme feelings for her until now; she'd never felt as loved even with such violence.

In her confused state, she reasoned that he had hit her because he cared so much; he had hit Joey because he loved her. In that moment, she knew she could never bear for him to be with other girls. She would have to be his lover now, too.

Unfortunately, she didn't comprehend that James had somehow changed in those moments when he had perceived that Beverly was making a fool of him. He would never be quite the same with her. Now he would be the one in control of the situation. Never again would she tell him what to do.

Beverly's most difficult decision now was when to capitulate to James' demands. She lost many nights of sleep that week wondering and wishing she had someone to confide in about her next move. Ironically, in the decision to become more intimate with James, she had lost him as a confidante; he would not be approachable in this situation.

Laura would never understand the dilemma facing Beverly, either. Laura had never been involved in a serious relationship and remained a virgin. Beverly knew Laura would talk her out of it, and Beverly didn't want that.

By Monday, Coach had heard about the party, of course. He tread carefully because he did not want James upset, but he did call him into his office after practice that day.

"James, what's this I hear about you and Beverly after the game Friday night?"

"What did you hear?" James responded cautiously.

"Well, that you two had a little fight and then went outside together for a good deal of time."

"Yeah, that's about it. Don't worry, Coach. Nothing will stand in our way of winning this weekend."

"Well, I sure hope so. We're so close now, James. I'd hate to see you blow it."

"Coach, it wouldn't be me that would blow it, now would it? It'd be those other important people who keep you in a job, right?"

"Right, James. I'm glad you understand."

"Oh, I understand just fine."

James left the office shaking his head at Coach Hoover's barely concealed worry over his relationship with Beverly. This town must really be scared of him or at least of his color, he thought as he walked back to the locker room for his shower.

Later, Beverly met him outside in the gym parking lot. She had her father's car, but she didn't have to be home for another hour. Beverly told him that she could drive him home. They decided to sit for a few moments in the darkening winter light before heading out into the night. They were in the shadows with the car barely visible from Coach Hoover's back office door. His blue Toronado was still parked there, but they watched as the lights in his office switched off. Several minutes later the outside light also went off, and Coach appeared in the doorway.

"James, what's Coach going to say if he sees us here?" Beverly asked as they watched Coach walk to his car.

"He can't see us over here, Beverly, if we just sit still. He'll think the car just belongs to one of the guys who is out riding with someone else."

Coach went to the passenger door of his car and opened it and then went around to the other side and got in, but the passenger door was still open. He reached up to the dome light and switched it off. Soon Karen Adams appeared in the doorway and dashed for the car slamming the door shut behind her. James and Beverly could see the two heads come close together since their eyes had very keenly adjusted to the dark shadows. Then Karen's head disappeared from view as Coach started the car and drove away looking as if he rode alone.

James let out a slow explosion of breath. "So, it's true! Man, that jerk. He just had me in his office warning me about you again and here he is screwing around with jail bait!"

"Boy, I hope my dad never hears about this one. Karen's been working at the furniture store in the evenings, cleaning up and dusting. He thinks she's a nice girl," Beverly gasped.

"Well, Beverly, just think of what we saw as insurance. Let's not tell anyone, but let's remember it, if we need it."

They pulled out of the parking lot with their secret safe between them.

The basketball team easily won the next round of play. They became the regional champs and would be playing in Lansing's Civic Center for the quarter finals on the next weekend.

Beverly had decided that if the team won Regionals, she would allow James whatever he wanted that very night. She prepared for the evening carefully since VHS was almost certain to win.

She waited with the crowd outside the locker room after the triumphant team returned from Lansing. She had on her best Bobbie Brooks, a favorite outfit of James because it made her blue eyes sparkle and brought out all the shiny highlights of her long blonde hair. And because she knew this was a night by which to mark the passage of a time in her life, she had spent hours on her appearance. Her hair glowed under the lights in the school lobby as did the ribbons carefully placed to hold the sides of her hair back off her face.

James noticed her right away when he emerged with the rest of the players from the locker room. He was pleased with the way she looked; he had a feeling tonight would be different with Beverly. He knew she was driven crazy with thoughts of him with someone else. And he could tell something was different about her in the way she looked at him, excited and scared all in one glance.

James decided that tonight he would ask one of his buddies if he could borrow his car. James was the only starter on the team without a car even though he lived the furthest away. Those other boys received their cars mostly that winter from their parents as a reward for being on a championship team. However, the star, the reason for the championship team, was forced to beg rides and on occasion asked to borrow a car. If James noticed this discrepancy, he never said a word. The other boys noticed and perhaps this was why they never denied James when he asked.

So on this special night, James approached Harry, one of the teams' guards. He agreed to let James borrow his Impala for the evening since he was double dating with Rick, the other guard. The couples could use Rick's car.

After some of the crowd had dispersed from in front of the locker room, James approached Beverly and told her she was coming with him. There was no need for her to say yes or no; the command was given, and she followed.

At this point, neither cared who saw that they left the school together. After the scene at last week's party, everyone was fairly certain that James and Beverly were seeing each other anyway. James was confident because he had an insurance policy on Coach, and besides they were so close to winning the state championship that he knew anyone who tried to keep him from playing at this point would themselves be run out of town. The team had become too big a deal for the gamblers in the surrounding area. No one would publicly admit it, but most other adult fans were already placing heavy bets on the outcome of the state game still two weeks away.

The clear and balmy night, unusual for early March in Michigan, brought a false hope for an end to the long frigid nights. It wouldn't last long. March always seemed to end in an avalanche of snow. Through the calm night, James and Beverly rode in silence with the windows down. She slid over next to him as they drove out into the country. Soon James found a pull–off spot on a dirt road overlooking a pasture. There were no houses on this road so if they saw anyone it would only be someone with the same thing on their minds. The unwritten parking code insisted it was first come, first use, so the newcomers would search for an unoccupied spot.

"It's really simpler this way, Beverly," James said as he drew her close to him. "But if we want to get it right, we need to get into the back seat. It'll be more comfortable."

Beverly, far too scared at this point to resist or even to say anything or even to wonder if James really cared if she was comfortable or not, obeyed. James knew what to do, she thought through a haze of nerves. She decided to put her faith and trust in him. He really did care for her, and she further reasoned, he would never hurt her.

Beverly's initiation to sex, supposedly a special moment in a girl's life, mimicked thousands of other women who lose their virginity to men with more concern for their own desires and satisfactions than the woman's.

James had never been with a virgin before. He actually didn't even consider that it would be different than his encounters with those other girls. Nor did he consider that his size might be uncomfortable for Beverly. He thought something was wrong with her when he began to have difficulties.

It didn't stop him, however, and he certainly didn't hear or maybe even comprehend her muffled sobs. And he didn't think to mumble words of endearment in her ears as he went about the business of entering her. He didn't even kiss her. Gentleness was no longer a word in his vocabulary as he met such strong resistance. His difficulty even made him angry at Beverly who just lay there whimpering; and so he became rougher.

Soon it was over for him, and he started dressing and moving toward the front seat while Beverly lay there wounded and wet. He did throw back a tissue.

"Here clean yourself up, Bev, and then get dressed, and for god's sake, blow your nose!" James yelled at her from the front seat.

Sniffling and moving slowly she did as he commanded.

When she finished she came back to the front seat.

"I'm sorry, James. It'll be better next time, I promise," Beverly tearfully told him.

"Sure, baby, don't worry about it. You'll do better next time." He put the car in reverse and pulled from their parking spot.

They drove home in silence, each wrapped in his and her own thoughts. James was curiously unsatisfied. It seemed something was missing because he felt empty on the inside, and this feeling he blamed on Beverly.

She felt numb; it certainly wasn't what she had imagined, and she also blamed herself. Donna had acted as if she had enjoyed what she had done with James. Why was it different for her when she loved him? She would try harder next time, although that thought brought a fresh stab of pain to her wounds, inside and out. She vowed to ignore the pain.

James managed to kiss her good night a block from her house where he parked the car. Beverly told him she would try harder next time, which seemed to please him. They agreed on one thing; Beverly needed to make some changes. Neither thought of any other reason for the lack of excitement and love in their first encounter.

And so Beverly dragged herself painfully from the car walking the darkened block to her house with a lowered head and feeling like a failure as a person and so inadequate as a woman. And James drove off into the night to find a more satisfying and willing partner.

CHAPTER TEN

After the regional win, the team won the quarter final game by crushing a team from Redford Township. The Detroit News ranked Victoria number one in the final high school Class C poll as the team won its 22nd consecutive game before a crowd of over 3,000. Even though James only scored 14 points in the game, he still managed 26 rebounds mostly under Redford's basket while also blocking nine of their shots.

Next the team took on Battle Creek Springfield in the semi–finals with James scoring a game–high record of 31 points. The final score of 95–61 included great plays by Harry and Rick as they both scored in the double figures.

The fervor in town reached its peak as the team prepared for the Saturday afternoon state championship game in Crisler Arena at the University of Michigan in Ann Arbor.

VHS had been picked during the week by The Detroit Free Press as the favorite to win. That prediction brought the TV reporters from Ann Arbor, Lansing, and Detroit to this small town and assured that the game would be covered on the channels received in Victoria. However, no one cared much about whether it was on TV or not; they wanted to see the game in living color. All the fans who had suddenly become fans late in the year and those fans who had bet heavily on the outcome of the final game made sure to get their tickets first, with little consideration for the high school students.

A tiny scandal erupted the week before the game when the number of tickets sent to VHS proved inadequate to seat all the students. The Detroit News reported this phenomenon as well as the fact that all the townspeople seemed to have enough tickets. The teams' classmates might be reduced to viewing the game at home on TV. The day after the article appeared, the school anonymously received enough tickets for all the students who wanted to attend.

James and Beverly continued their meetings in back seats of cars during the two weeks between regionals and state. Beverly learned to relax more, mainly because she felt she was giving something to James that he needed. Her confidence that he loved her grew even though he had never said it in those exact words. Further, her false sense of bravado allowed her to imagine that his contact with other girls no longer existed.

They had decided that after the final game they would approach her parents and announce that they would be seeing each other on a regular basis. They talked about marriage when James embarked on his professional career. They didn't use words like going steady; they felt that they were different and more grown up than their peers.

As long as Beverly played by his rules, James was satisfied and happy with her. She was trying so hard to please him in every way, and he knew it. This effort alone gave him a perverse satisfaction, although not sexually. For that he had chosen carefully a girl he could always see after he had dropped off Beverly. A girl whose parents did not keep close tabs on her. In fact, Sally's mother had just died, and her father was dating a woman in Williamston. Sally was the only one at home and many nights her father didn't even come home. Her accessibility attracted James and provided sustenance for his starving body. Lonely, willing, and closed–mouthed, she fed him willingly.

However, he wanted Beverly to make a strong public commitment to him. It would be a test of her loyalty to him. The only way to assure her constancy to him required her to break her attachment to the Canons. He knew Beverly was naive in regards to the reaction of their announcement. She had told him they would balk at first because he didn't belong to any particular church. She told him they might be upset because he hadn't been baptized in the Methodist Church.

They decided that after the game, James and his teammates would rent a few motel rooms in Ann Arbor for a party with just their girlfriends. On the sly, one of the local men involved with the gambling, had palmed over a hundred dollar bill to each of the five starters the night before the game. Each promised to use the money only after they were the state's champs. They decided to rent the rooms and have their own private party to end one hell of a season.

Beverly sat in the stands nearly bursting with pride. Even though most of her friends suspected a relationship between her and James, Beverly didn't talk about it. She would have loved to tell them and brag about how much the star loved her, but she kept her silence. However, in the frenzy of the state game it became obvious to everyone around her that Beverly acted much more animated than usual in her shouts down to the court. No one missed it either when James turned in her direction during a time out in the game and threw her a smile and slight wave. Everyone noticed the blush and pleased smile that crossed her face.

Even though Laura, sitting next to her in the bleachers, kept prodding her, she kept her silence; after tonight they would all know, and she would wait to share her news.

The game seemed almost anticlimactic because victory was theirs so easily. It was not much of a contest since they won by 20 points. However, when Coach Hoover rode on the shoulders of his players around the perimeters of the court, the excitement returned. The team smiled and raised one finger in the air as they posed for all of Michigan's major newspapers and TV stations.

James was most sought after and forced to answer the reporters inane questions before heading off to the showers. He didn't mind the attention, but he was grateful that the press was banned from the locker rooms. There, they imbibed in the liquor brought in by the happy locals. Even Coach didn't mind; his job ended that night for the next eight months, and the job remained secure as his win record had just soared to unbelievable heights. He might not have rested so easily if he knew the real reason that James had been regarding him with disdain the last two weeks.

Beverly waited patiently for James after the game in the lobby of Crisler Arena. She waited with the other girlfriends; Beverly had known them all her life so conversation continued between them, although each girl wondered privately why Beverly remained with them. They all knew now that the rumors of James and her must be true; she wasn't waiting for anyone else, they figured, because everyone else's girlfriend was there. They were going to be privy to some pretty juicy news especially if she was coming to the motel with them. They may not have been conscious of any maliciousness in their souls, but they did understand they were the first to know for sure. Already they anticipated calling the girls in their group tomorrow, and they imagined what they would say. To be sure every one of the girls would be watching closely tonight even as they snuggled with their own personal heroes.

Finally the boys arrived, and Beverly raced into James' waiting arms in front of all the team. It didn't matter anymore, and besides they weren't really conscious of what they did or didn't do.

"Hey, baby, you look great," James told her as he lifted her off the ground in a celebratory hug.

"I'm so proud of you, James," Beverly cooed as she kissed his ear before he set her carefully on the ground.

"Well, hey, you guys, what are we standing around here for?" James asked when he noticed everyone just standing there and staring at the two of them.

"Yeah, let's go," Greg said as he headed out the revolving doors of the arena.

James' satisfaction with life and Beverly shown brightly in his face and for that one moment he felt that everything might be possible for him. Why not? He had certainly received his share of adulation in the last few months and tonight was the culmination of all his effort. He was the best, and now he had the best.

However, he didn't quite trust Beverly yet, but he was proud of the way she looked and acted most of the time when she obeyed him. The last two weeks had shown him his power over her, and he felt gratified by her acceptance and presence. It was the icing on his own personal cake.

When they all arrived at the motel, it became obvious that the boys had figured it all out beforehand. They paid for three adjoining rooms for the night. One room would be for general partying. The beer, ice, and whiskey set up on the dresser indicated that the partying would commence here. All the chairs from the other two rooms had been placed here also. The other rooms with two double beds apiece were for couples. No lights were allowed on in those rooms so everyone could have some privacy.

James and Beverly socialized a bit with two other couples who weren't all that anxious to adjourn to the outer rooms. James even brought Beverly a beer and coaxed her into a sip of whiskey. He had been thinking lately that maybe Beverly just needed to relax before they had sex. After all, he usually had been drinking before, and it loosened him up a bit, he reasoned. He supposed as long as he controlled the amount she drank, it would be all right. Beverly did relax and even felt comfortable in the presence of Kris and Mary Jane even though she knew they couldn't wait until they could tell someone about James and her. Beverly didn't care; let them talk. Her parents would know soon, and then she could tell everyone that James wanted to marry her.

After waiting a reasonable amount of time, and as couples drifted back into the party room, James and Beverly retired to the room on the right. For the time being it was empty, and they could have some privacy. This would be the first time they had ever been in a bed together and somehow they both were more excited about the prospect.

As they lay in the bed, Beverly felt an arousal inside of her that had not been there before. She worried about making James enjoy his time with her, and her need to care for him created an excitement for her. She began to enjoy the way he touched her, even though it wasn't always gentle. Tonight, however, he seemed to be taking his time and spent more moments exploring her body as if he had never felt it before. Beverly began to slow down and enjoy the caresses when suddenly she felt swept away by emotion and shuddered throughout her whole body. She didn't even know that she had just achieved her first orgasm. James didn't know it either; he just felt overwhelmed that she seemed to be enjoying herself so much

70

for the first time. It made him feel softer towards her; and therefore, he became gentler, which in turn relaxed Beverly even more as she shuddered once more.

They forgot the rest of the world and in particular the rest of the party. They didn't notice when another couple entered the room and the other bed. They didn't notice the sounds they made in their own nest; and they definitely didn't notice that they had shocked everyone in those three motel rooms with their love.

The others all thought that what James and Beverly were doing was far more outrageous than what they had in mind. These Victoria children had been trained and conditioned to stick with their own kind and so the shock came from the difference of the two people in the back room. And besides Beverly belonged to them; somehow it seemed she had betrayed them and their whole life. The boys looked closely at their girlfriends to detect signs that they might also be capable of such treachery. Although they, as Beverly, had been taught that there was no difference between races, they had also learned that everyone was happier when living with their own kind. Somehow that lesson had not reached Beverly; and therefore, she did not consider that she was doing anything wrong. For her, she was doing everything right. She loved James, and he loved her, and all was right in her world for the moment.

On the way back to Victoria late that night, James and Beverly made plans in the back seat of Rick's car. They both knew now that their relationship was serious; they had every intention of making it stronger.

"You know we could get married after the season next year," James suggested quietly in the back seat of Harry's car as they sped back to Victoria late that night.

"I'd like that. Where'd we live?" Beverly asked.

"Wherever I get a basketball scholarship. We can live in married housing and you can finish high school there, or not."

"I just want to be with you, James, that's all. I want to have your babies," she whispered into his ear.

"Hey, baby, one step at a time, but I want that, too." He

71

kissed her softly. Tonight he felt he owned her and the rest of the world.

They continued planning and cuddling and whispering in the dark as the car sped north on Highway 52 back to the confines of Victoria.

They also decided that James would show up at her house on Sunday after church and dinner. She would introduce him and together they would explain their relationship to her parents. Beverly looked forward to welcoming James into her family. And she just knew they would learn to love him as much as she did.

CHAPTER ELEVEN

Beverly slept soundly and deeply that night. A contentedness seemed to have enveloped her and acted as a heavy tranquilizer.

It was a sleep that was needed for the coming disaster; a calamity of disturbing proportions. For while Beverly slept, others did not. Never had the Victorian phone lines worked at such late night ferocity as friends called friends. For example, Mary Jane, who couldn't wait until the morning, called her friend, Diane. Diane's mom overheard some of the conversation between Mary Jane and her daughter. Immediately she questioned her about the situation. Diane, never good at lying and always good at gossip, blurted out that James Kelly and Beverly Canon had spent the night together in a motel room in Ann Arbor. Mrs. Thomas' head snapped back as if attached to her shoulders with only a rubber band.

Without much thought, Mrs. Thomas went to the phone to call May Randall, Martha Canon's sister, to break the news. The standard procedure in Victoria for such a disaster required that the gossip should go to the family preferably on the wings of good–intentioned friends. Mrs. Thomas refrained from calling the Canons herself. That would have been breaking the town's code of spreading the news. The passing of information must occur in a logical sequence. In this case, the logical sequence required another transmitter. Mrs. Thomas was not close enough as a friend or relative to directly relay the news to Mrs. Canon. Therefore, a third person, closer to the family, must be told the details, and then they would decide who would carry the information and when. Of course, all of this telling contained only the best of Christian intentions.

Beginning to think more clearly, Mrs. Thomas replaced the receiver and decided to wait until morning to spread the news of the horrible events of the past evening. Might as well let everyone else get one good night's rest, she thought.

73

May Randall began breaking the eggs for the morning meal when the phone rang. Probably Doris Stanhope calling to say she was ill, and she'd have to teach the third grade Sunday school class as well as her own fourth grade class, she mused as she reluctantly reached for the phone. As her son JJ grew, she had worked somewhat on improving her reputation so he could be a part of the inner social circles of Victoria. One of the ways she rehabilitated herself concerned activities within the church. Luckily for her, her family's position in the Methodist Church gave her a foothold in the door, and the rest she accomplished by attending the woman's circle every Wednesday and teaching Sunday School each week. It didn't seem to do JJ much good, however, since he had chosen to follow in his father's mostly renegade footsteps. She also curtailed her affairs when she would travel out of town occasionally for her moments of escape. Lately she hadn't even wanted to do that as thoughts of Hollis kept invading her consciousness.

"May, I hope you're sitting down because I have some extremely disturbing news that concerns one of your family," Betty Thomas began in her best funeral–home voice.

"Goodness, Betty! What has happened? Is someone dead?" Already the older family members names began running through her mind.

"No one is dead yet, but there will be trouble when this news gets out. My Diane got a call last night from Mary Jane Daniels who goes with Kris Gerald who's on the basketball team and. . ."

"Good heavens, Betty! What has all this got to do with my family? I'm trying to get my eggs scrambled. . ."

"Last night after the game in Ann Arbor, your niece Beverly, went to a motel room alone with James Kelly, that's what this nonsense has to do with your family!!!" screamed Betty, unable to keep the news any longer.

Silence, deadly silence, followed. The shock of the news took a moment to sink in and even longer before May began flaring her nostrils.

"May, are you still there? Did you hear me?"

74

Clearing her throat, May asked who had seen Beverly and James together.

"Mary Jane and Kris saw them go into a room together," replied Betty, not even caring why or how Mary Jane and Kris saw this phenomena themselves.

"Who else knows?" came May's dread–filled question as she pondered containment.

"All I know is that Mary Jane called my Diane last night when she got home, and I overheard them talking."

It was bad, very bad, May thought quickly.

"Well, thanks for seeing fit to let the family know, Betty. I'll take care of it on this end. Just don't call anyone else. Something like this needs to be dealt with privately until it blows over. Maybe it's not true anyway. I just hate to be the one to tell my poor sister. She's had enough heartbreak the past two years alone to last a lifetime."

Betty assured her she would keep quiet, and the two women hung up the receivers. May stood next to the phone for a very long time before picking it up again. She would call a family conference at the Canons' house. She called her other sister Connie and her nephew George who lived in Victoria. She thought George's presence would help his parents after the news was broken. After making those calls, she telephoned her sister.

"Martha, I have a little problem I need to discuss with you and Hollis this morning. Do you think you could stay home from church? Send Beverly on by herself; she really doesn't need to be around to hear about my problems," May requested.

"May, is everything all right?"

"I just need to talk to you and Hollis. Can you stay home just this once?"

"Of course, but if it's that important to you, can't you tell me what it's about?"

"Not over the phone, Martha. I'll be there in 45 minutes."

May quickly hung up before Martha could ask anything more of her. She was not about to tell her over the phone without

75

back up. She was worried about her sister, but she worried about Hollis more. Hollis never handled controversial situations well even though he dealt with the business of death on a daily basis. May knew how Hollis dealt with that and unfortunately Martha wouldn't have whiskey in the house to help him cope with this situation. She wondered, not for the first time, how their lives might be different if she hadn't made some costly mistakes so many years before as her thoughts drifted back over time.

Hollis had been in love with May Stuart from the moment he first laid on eyes on her petite but well–rounded body and perfectly formed face. May liked the fact that Hollis would someday own a funeral home and furniture store. She didn't look much further than leaving the crowded parsonage as soon as she could.

"Would you mind awfully living next door to the funeral home, May?" Hollis asked one winter's night under a starless sky while sitting in his old Model A outside of the parsonage.

They had been discussing the future, and marriage became a logical choice for the direction of the conversation.

"No, Hollis, it wouldn't bother me. Maybe we could add on a room or two, and I could put some new furniture in the house once your Uncle Paul leaves. They will leave, won't they, when he retires and turns the business over to you?"

"Yes, that's the plan. They've always wanted a small place in the country so they already have the land; they'll probably start building the year I apprentice."

"Well, that's good. You know, we'll need lots of privacy, Hollis. What about your mother? Where will she live?"

"Why, Mom? She'll live with us, of course, dear. My brother will be off to college and beginning his own life by the time we marry, so we won't need to worry about him, but Mom wouldn't have anywhere else to stay."

Now May didn't like this idea one bit, but she knew better than to pursue the topic anymore that night. She liked Hollis all right, but she really loved his money and what it could bring her. She already envisioned the entertaining she would do, how she would be dressed, and the table she would set.

Having her mother–in–law under foot would put a damper on this business, she was certain. Already Mrs. Canon made remarks about unnecessary expenditures of money and frivolous purchases, and they weren't even engaged yet. May would work on this situation over the next few months. She knew Hollis would eventually see the sense in her proposal in building her mother a separate place closer to the furniture store in town or even buying her the old house across from the store. One thing remained constant in May's mind; her future mother–in–law would not reside in the house with them as they began their married life.

And so during the following year in which Hollis finished up high school and prepared to go to the University of Detroit to study the art of embalming, May's campaign began. First, she would sigh and wonder out loud how she would manage a nursery in the small house with her mother–in–law taking up one of the crucial rooms. Or she would pull back from Hollis' embrace and stare languidly at him from half–closed eyes and mention how much she looked forward to being married to him when she could show him exactly how she felt. But then a cloud would pass over her face until Hollis would ask what was wrong.

"Oh, nothing. I was just trying to imagine us in the bedroom with your mother right next door, but I'm sure we'll manage, dear."

Within six months, Hollis decided that his mother would need her own place when he married May. May tried to protest at first, but Hollis became adamant.

"No, May, we need to start our marriage right. We need time alone, and mother will be happier in her own place, I'm sure."

"Whatever you think is the right thing to do, Hollis."

And May smiled privately to herself in the way that women for centuries have smiled when they've convinced their mate that an idea born in the woman's mind was the sole invention of the man's.

Hollis went away to Detroit for his year's study in the fall of 1941. He came home once a month and spent most of his time with May who wasn't exactly sitting home idle while she waited.

77

A new boy had moved to Victoria that year and his father had opened up the new Ford dealership on the outskirts of town. Johnny Randall was as handsome as May was beautiful and as rich as Hollis, if not richer. And he was a bad boy. Right away they noticed one another and before long they couldn't keep their hands off one another. But May continued to string along Hollis because Johnny didn't seem like the marrying kind even though he had convinced May to do married kinds of things in the back seat of the newly built Lincoln. Never before had Detroit produced such a luxury vehicle, and Johnny's was one of only a few thousand produced. That attracted May beyond measure. However, above all else, May intended to be married to someone when she graduated in June of 1942 and so far Hollis was the only one who had proposed.

One weekend in early December, Hollis made an unannounced visit to Victoria. He had just been home the weekend before and sensed that something was wrong with May. Even though he had to work in the lab late that Friday night, he drove the 70 miles home anyway to see May and try to find out the source of her troubles.

He pulled up in front of the parsonage at about 10:00 p.m. No lights were on inside except the back porch light which meant one of the children was still out. Curiously he saw that Johnny Randall's Lincoln was parked on the side street of the parsonage, and the windows were all steamed up.

He had met Johnny a couple of months ago at a party and took an instant dislike to him. Now what could he possibly be doing here at this hour?

Hollis pulled up close behind the car leaving his headlights on. Two heads popped up in the back seat as he walked closer to the car. He gazed in amazement through the side windows at the naked flesh appearing before him. Finally he looked further into the car and saw that one of the heads resembled May. The two began grabbing for clothes strewn about the car, but Hollis had already figured out the situation and was in his car backing carefully away and never hearing May call after him. He drove all the way back to Detroit in stunned silence.

Two days later on December 7, 1941, the whole country buzzed with news of war as Hollis felt his life crumbling around him. Early Monday morning, he went to the recruiting office and enlisted. His status as a student studying a science put him in the medic crew, and he left for Europe just before Christmas. He came home once to visit his distraught mother who felt Hollis should have waited to see if his status as a student would exempt him from the war. He studiously avoided May and the parsonage and the church before shipping out.

May got married in 1942 all right, but she never graduated from high school. The wedding took place in April at the home of the Randalls. The Stuarts didn't attend, but Johnny Randall, Junior's birth the following September healed the hurt somewhat between May and her family as she presented her parents with their first grandchild.

When Hollis came home in 1945, sadder and more gaunt, the light seemed to have disappeared from his face, and he never smiled. He retained his slim physique and muscular tone with endless games of tennis that summer. However, he looked older than his years with deep frown lines on his forehead and around his mouth.

His uncle decided to just put him into apprenticeship right away since he and his wife had postponed their retirement until the war ended and Hollis returned home. He spent a lot of time in the basement of the funeral home that year of his apprenticeship and puzzling his mother and uncle, he even spent time down there when no dead bodies presented themselves. The embalmment of Hollis had begun in earnest. Within a year of his return, he and Martha were married with his mother living in the spare bedroom of their house.

Martha Canon hung up the phone and turned to her husband. "May's on her way over. She needs to talk to us about a problem, and would rather not have Beverly here. I imagine Johnny's done something again. I sure hope he didn't hit her this time."

Hollis looked up from the Sunday papers and thoughtfully gazed at Martha who had gained a considerable amount of weight since their marriage. Her plain beige housedress attempted to hide some of the mounds of flesh. Her hair, turning gray in spots, always defied the pins which attempted to hold it in place. Even though she could afford nicer clothes and a weekly hair stylist, she never liked spending money on herself. She couldn't see any reason since she would never be as beautiful as May.

In contrast, the years had brought a distinguished look to Hollis' worn face. He had never gained much weight even with middle age although he had long ago given up tennis. His blonde hair had gradually turned white giving him the aura of a venerable statesman.

Hollis hoped Johnny hadn't done anything at all to May. Over the years, with continued close contact with May, he had forgiven her and almost forgotten completely the picture of her bare thighs in the window of Johnny's Lincoln.

When he did remember, he forgot Johnny Randall's presence and only felt a longing to be the person between those lithe limbs even after all these years. Unfortunately, he couldn't forgive himself for allowing her to marry that son of a bitch and not fighting for her like a real man.

He took a long sigh and went back to the obituary page to look over the competition's ads.

CHAPTER TWELVE

James didn't fare as well as Beverly in the sleep department. A feeling of uneasiness crept slowly up through his chest into his head leaving him shaky and nervous. When he finally left his bed and dressed for the day ahead, he chastised himself for his nervousness. Determined to remain calm, he begged a ride to Victoria from his sister who had come for a weekend visit after taking his mother to the game the night before. He arrived in town just as Beverly left church. His sister dropped him off near the sidewalk where Beverly stood.

She looked so cheerful and hopeful and beautiful and clean in a new pink dress. James felt the compunction to burst her bubble and her happiness.

"That's an ugly dress, baby," James said languidly between half–closed eyes.

Beverly looked at him at first with a grin, and then surprise as she realized he meant the remark or at least meant to wound her with the remark. She said nothing.

"Why are you just standing here? Getting scared the old Canon clan won't like their all white baby girl dirtied by this big black boy?"

"James, why are you acting this way?" Beverly finally asked.

"What way? Just because you're getting scared about bringing me home to momma?"

"Let's go. Mom and Dad stayed home from church to deal with some problem of Aunt May's. Probably her husband beat her up last night. We'll just go in the house and see what happens from there, OK?" Beverly tried not to let her fear of James' behavior show. She was immediately sorry she mentioned her aunt's domestic troubles.

81

"OK, but don't expect me to get an invitation to dinner."
James threw his arm around her shoulder, and they began the trek to
the Canon's house on Main Street.

From several blocks away, Beverly could see two extra cars
in the driveway. She expected Aunt May's but not the others. Something big must have happened to have kept the aunts home from
church. In puzzlement she led James forward down the sidewalk.

Inside the house, the quiet permeated every corner although
the silence seemed like the quiet before a tornado; that moment when
everyone should be heading for shelter, and the quiet sounds like a
roar because of the devastation soon to follow.

"Hollis, Martha, I have something to tell you," May had
begun. "It's about Beverly."

"What about Beverly?" Martha asked.

"I got a call this morning. Evidently Beverly and James
Kelly went together to a motel room after last night's game," May
said looking directly at Martha who sat on the couch next to Hollis.

"No, I don't believe it. Who told you this?" Martha rose
from her seat with clenched fists.

"Betty Thomas called. Her daughter told her."

"He must have kidnapped her. Beverly wouldn't do such a
thing, she's a good girl, isn't she, Hollis?" Martha started to cry.

"Now, Martha, let's talk to Beverly first. There's probably
some explanation," Hollis finally said. He didn't go to his wife, but
he looked at May for some word. "May, did she say anything else?"

"No, not really. Some of the kids know. That's how her
daughter found out. But, you're right, Hollis, you need to wait to talk
to Beverly before jumping to conclusions." She gave him a slight
smile and walked to the couch and patted his shoulder.

"I didn't even know she knew James Kelly," Martha said
from the corner of the living room. "Why would Beverly go out with
someone like him when she could date any boy in Victoria?"

Martha Canon remained adamant that Beverly was the most
beautiful and most popular girl at Victoria High. She liked to imagine that her only daughter possessed all the qualities that she never

had.

The more Hollis thought about May's news the more upset he became. Hollis began pacing while his son, George attempted to talk to him.

"Dad, let's just wait to hear Beverly's side. Maybe it's all untrue like Mom says or maybe there's a logical explanation."

"A logical explanation for walking into a motel room with him? I doubt it!" Hollis muttered as he continued to wear out the carpet.

"Beverly has better sense than to get mixed up with someone like him," Martha interjected. "Why I've heard that he drinks and does things that just aren't accepted in Victoria." Finally the nostrils began their ritual.

The loud explosion came from George who had started looking out the front window. Out on the sidewalk stood James and Beverly holding hands and talking very intently. The house slanted as the whole group in the living room ran to the window to see what had made George yell so frightfully. The quiet began again, but the faces went ahead and turned beet red anyway. George ran to the front door and flung it open upon the two young lovers on the porch now.

"What are doing here, George? Where're Susan and the boys?" Beverly innocently asked. "Did you go to Saturday night mass?"

"You know exactly why I'm here. Get that son of a bitch out of here," George screamed.

Beverly stood rooted to the spot. Her favorite brother had never raised his voice to anyone let alone her. Why was he acting this way?

James didn't need to ask that question as he began to back away. Beverly grabbed his arm and pleaded for him to stay.

"Don't listen to him, James. Let's find out what's going on here."

Beverly tried to pull James into the house, but he resisted.

George came up very close to the two of them, "Beverly, get him out of here. He can't come into the house. I can't guarantee that

Dad won't try to kill him. Now let him go and come into the house with me."

James pulled her hand off of his arm and nodded his head. "He's right, Bev. Go on in by yourself and find out what's going on. We'll talk later."

"What is going on here! Why can't James come into my house with me?" screamed Beverly as she watched James walk down the sidewalk.

He didn't turn around but walked away with his head high. He had warned Beverly this would happen yet he had wanted to believe her when she denied it.

George gave her a push into the house, and then right into the middle of the living room. Everyone just stared at her.

Finally Hollis broke the silence. "What's wrong with you, Beverly? Why would you do such a thing with him."

"What are you talking about? Do what with him?"

May and Connie quickly began gathering their coats and whispering their goodbyes to Martha. Hollis, George, and Beverly remained rooted to their spots.

"We know where you were last night and what you were doing there," announced George finally.

"Oh, and what was that? Would you mind telling me what that was?" Again, Beverly's voice reached the higher octaves.

"Beverly, we don't need to spell it out for you. We know. Did you ever think about what you were doing to me? What if you should get pregnant by that boy?" Martha said quietly and sadly.

"If I did get pregnant, we would get married now instead of later."

"What do you mean?" Mrs. Canon said quietly.

"I mean that James and I were headed in here today to announce that we are seeing one another and will be getting married in a few years."

"Over my dead body," Hollis Canon angrily announced.

"Why are all of you so against James?"

"He's just not a good person, Beverly. We've heard things

84

about him that just don't fit with the kind of boy we want you to date. Now you are going to have to break it off with him today over the phone. We don't want you to see him, and we certainly don't want him over here again." Mrs. Canon made this statement all in one single breath while Beverly stared incredulously at her mother.

"You don't like James because he is black," Beverly retorted.

"That's not it at all! Your father and I have raised you better than that, Beverly."

"You are prejudiced and worried about what the rest of Victoria will think if you let your daughter date a black person, just like James said."

"Beverly, you can stop this nonsense right now. We've given you our reasons for not dating this boy, and that's all we're going to say on the subject." Mr. Canon had lost his patience and would not tolerate his daughter's disrespectful accusations.

Beverly just stomped her way into her bedroom where she slammed the door shut with one swift kick. This time her father did not make her get up off the bed and shut the door properly as he usually did when she threw a temper tantrum. As Beverly plotted about what to do next, her parents and George talked about their next step.

"She needs therapy. She is not thinking straight. He's done this to her. I could call that clinic where Dave received counseling and see what they recommend," Mrs. Canon said as a last resort.

"She doesn't need therapy. She just needs a good paddling," Hollis said angrily.

"Come on, Dad. She's beyond that. I agree with Mom, get her some help," George carefully approached his father.

"It's just not natural! What's wrong with that girl?" Hollis yelled. "He's not one of us!"

"Hollis, calm down. We'll find out what happened just like with Dave, and everything will be all right," Martha came up to him and rested her head on his back.

Finally, Hollis sighed in resignation. "All right, but I don't like it. Make the call," he said as he sat back down on the couch to retrieve the Sunday papers.

"I guess I'll go on home. Susan is probably worried sick. She thinks of Beverly as her own sister. Maybe she could try talking to her," George said to his mother.

"Good idea, George. Give Susan and the boys our love."

As George pulled out of the driveway, Mrs. Canon remarked, "Susan is good for him even if she is a Catholic."

Beverly carefully packed a few things into her large purse and waited. Finally her parents announced through the closed door that they were walking up to Grandma Stuart's house and would be back in an hour or so. Beverly came into the living room and called Laura, her only friend.

"I need a place to crash tonight. Can I come over?"

"Sure, my folks are out until late so they probably won't even know you're here. Come on over," was the welcome reply.

Without leaving a note, Beverly walked out of the house and down the street to her friend's house. She hadn't made any plans past that evening, but she knew she couldn't stay in the same house with her parents tonight.

When her parents returned, it didn't take Hollis long to find Beverly. It was a process of elimination and a matter of minutes before he showed up on the steps of Laura's house to pull his only daughter out and put her in the car.

"Don't you realize what you're doing to your mother?" These words were the only ones spoken by Hollis as he drove the short distance home.

Beverly didn't reply. How could she? Why did her mother always assume that the whole world existed to just mess things up for her? For someone with such low self–worth, she sure put herself at the center of the universe.

When she entered the house, she met her mother in the hallway.

"Tomorrow we are going to the clinic in Ann Arbor to see that you receive some counseling to help you see things more clearly," she announced.

Beverly began to protest but could see that it was no use. She would simply pull herself into her shell and not let the outside world in to see her wounds. She had done this all her life and so it took little practice to once again shield herself.

"And you need to get on the phone to that James boy right now so I can hear you break it off with him."

When Beverly didn't respond, Mrs. Canon picked up the phone's receiver and pushed it into Beverly's face.

"I can't do it with you standing here."

"Oh yes, you can, and you will."

Beverly slowly dialed the number she had never called but had memorized. James answered on the first ring.

"James, this is Beverly. My mother is making me call you. I'm not allowed to see you anymore. I have to break up with you and go to counseling so I can think more clearly." Beverly said in monotone.

"I told you so, Beverly," came the reply just before he hung up on her.

CHAPTER THIRTEEN

James returned the phone to its receiver and sat quietly for a moment. Then he picked up the phone again and dialed.

"Get out here and pick me up," he spoke tersely into the mouthpiece. Then he slammed the phone back down.

Sally picked him up in twenty minutes, but they didn't drive very far. Just down a deserted cow path not far from Ravens Woods. James didn't waste any time before taking his rage out on Sally. They didn't even get in the back seat. And Sally gave James everything he desired and for a moment, his rage subsided and removed itself to the outskirts of his mind. He received comfort and solace in the arms of this young girl who asked for nothing in return from him.

The next day at school, James didn't see Beverly in her usual spots. He had some things to say to her, and now she didn't even show up at school so he could let her know what would happen next. So he went to Sally's locker and talked her into going to her house for the day instead of staying at school.

Beverly and her parents drove to Ann Arbor the next morning to the clinic. The psychologist who had seen her brother recommended that Beverly attend a group therapy session specifically geared to troubled teens. The Canons quickly agreed, failing to ask Beverly her opinion. It no longer mattered what she thought; they remained convinced that Beverly had been brainwashed by James. She certainly wouldn't have thought to marry him on her own, not their daughter.

Beverly entered the session room wearing her Bobbie Brooks matching outfit with barrettes in place. The group sat around in a circle in metal folding chairs. The appearance of this anomaly into the room brought snickers from the torn jeans group already in their seats. Uncomfortably, she found a seat and looked around the circle. Why was she here? She didn't fit in with this group.

"Beverly, welcome to our group. We are just beginning. I'd like everyone to go around and introduce themselves and try in a sentence or two to explain what brings you to this group," the therapist explained.

"I'm Yogi. The court sent me here after my last bust. It's either this or sit in juvie with a bunch of criminals. All I did was sell a few joints."

"I'm Jessie. I'm also here on court order. I got busted lifting stereo headphones from Sears. My second offense."

"I'm Kelly. My dad just got arrested for having sex with me. When I got pregnant, everyone freaked because I'm only thirteen. They all wanted to know who the father was and finally I told them. Now they all think I need to work out some shit before the baby's born."

On and on these stories went with similar themes and attitudes until Beverly's turn.

She cleared her throat and honestly didn't know what to say. "My name's Beverly. And I don't know why I'm here except that I'm in love, and my parents are bigots."

The snickers soon turned into snide and rude comments about poor, little "Barbie" and what a tough life she must have. Finally the therapist intervened and began asking Kelly some questions about her incestuous baby.

Beverly removed herself mentally from this group as the issues of drug use, thievery, and rape became the main topic for the group. How much longer could she stand it? How would she manage to see James? She would talk with him at school the next day, and they would figure out something.

When she could finally leave, she told her parents, "I'm cured. Let's go home."

However, her parents made an appointment for the next week before leaving the clinic.

The next day, James spotted her walking in the back door of school. Angrily he walked towards her and grabbed her arm roughly.

"Let go of me, James. You're hurting me!"

"Hurting you? Hurting YOU! You haven't seen anything yet. I want to talk to you and get some things straight."

"I won't talk to you with you holding my arm like this," she managed to gasp.

He loosened his grip, and she began walking away from him. He saw her go into the girl's bathroom. Without much thought, he went in behind her and cleared the room. When they were alone, he backhanded her, the hit making its mark on her left cheek.

"Please, James, don't hit me anymore. I'll listen to you. Please, don't hurt me," she cried as she held her hands up to her face to shield herself against any further blows. He scared her when he was like this, but she understood why he hit her. And she deserved it, she thought as she looked at him as if she was a deer caught in the headlights of an oncoming vehicle.

"That's better. Now you listen to me, baby. Your parents reacted just as I told you they would. Now what are you going to do about that?" he demanded.

"I had to call you the other night, James. My mother was standing right there forcing the phone in my face. She stood there the whole time I spoke to you."

He raised his hand as if to strike her again and held it in mid–air over her face. "That's not what I asked you. What are you going to do about it?"

"I–I d–don't know what you mean," she wailed.

"I think you do. Are you still my girl?" He grabbed both of her arms and pulled her roughly toward him.

"Of course, I am! I haven't changed the way I feel about you! James, let's run away from here. My parents are making me go to this group therapy crap once a week and won't let me see you. Let's just go away from here now," she pleaded.

"Now we can't do that, Beverly. I've got to stay here one more year so I can at least get picked up by a college offering me the best deal. I can't go anywhere until that happens. We'll see each other, but you'll just have to be careful and figure out ways to get out of the house, now won't you, baby?" He really wasn't asking.

90

"OK, listen, James, I'm babysitting at the Brown's Friday night. You can come over there for a little while if you come in the back door. OK?"

"That'll work. See ya then. And hey, baby. . ."

"Yes, James?"

He pinched the tip of her left breast between his thumb and forefinger until she winced. "Save this for me," he commanded as he sailed out of the girls' bathroom leaving her behind.

Beverly's humiliation completed its cycle. She washed her face and checked for signs of bruising. None this time.

Around ten on Friday night, Beverly heard the slight knock on the back door of the Brown's house. When she opened the door, there stood James obviously high. His bloodshot eyes gave him away as did the sway in his upper body as he leaned down to give her a kiss.

"Hey, baby," he said softly as he grabbed her around the waist with one arm and pinched her right breast hard with the free hand.

"Oouh, that hurts, James," she cried.

"Oh, yeah, well how about this." He switched sides and pinched her other breast.

"James, leave me alone! You're hurting me!" She tried to break away from his grasp.

"You don't tell me what to do, girl. Haven't I taught you that already? Now come here, we've got some making up to do."

Again he swayed toward her as she walked into the dining room. He managed to grab the sleeve on her sweater and pulled her back into his arms. "Now, we're gonna figure out whosh boss," he slurred with nauseating beer breath.

"James, stop it! I don't want to do this! I'm babysitting. What if one of the kids wakes up? The Browns might come home early."

"Why are you always worrying about other people? Why don't you worry about me for once." And with that James gave her a shove into the living room right beside the front door. He then pulled her down onto the floor with him.

"Stop, James! We can't do this. Someone might walk in." She continued to plead with him, but he no longer heard her as he began the business of undoing his pants and pulling hers down.

In his drunken clumsiness, he finally managed to pin her down by holding both hands above her head and laying directly on top of her so she couldn't move. The smell of whiskey and marijuana nauseated Beverly as she slowly began to realize that she was powerless to fight him.

"Now we're going to do this whether ya want it or not and ya really want it doncha ya, baby?"

"No, James, please stop."

He squeezed her wrists harder and then thrust himself into her. She was not ready or open to him so he pushed harder and harder, ripping and tearing at her dry opening.

She no longer protested. The futility of her situation made her weak, and the fight swept out of her as she just lay there ignoring the pain and ignoring him. She retreated to her familiar shell knowing he would finish soon.

He continued hammering away at her body, but she firmly kept her eyes closed and went to that other place where no harm could come to her. She never thought she would have to go to that place with James, but she realized slowly that he was just like the others, and she had no where to turn. And worse, her family had caused his behavior.

As his breathing became more intense, the life seemed to drain right out of him. He lay on her body for long moments and almost passed out in that position. Beverly nudged him, and he rolled over allowing her to pull up her pants even though she could see blood between her legs and on the wood floor beneath her. James finally stood up and zipped his pants.

"When will you learn, baby, that it's always so much easier when you obey me? It doesn't have to be so hard, you know. Now clean yourself up, and I'll see ya later." And he walked out the front door into the waiting car.

Beverly lay on the floor for long moments, completely drained. Only the sound of a clock ticking and her deep breathing permeated the silence of the room. She had no tears to cry. She knew that now she had reached the never–ending bottom, the abyss. Her mind didn't acknowledge what had happened as a rape because after all she knew James and had been having sex with him for a few months. Besides tonight she let it happen and didn't fight back and even felt responsible for his behavior. Even though rape never entered her vocabulary on that dark night, she felt an incredible sinking feeling of despair and knew she had no one to blame but herself.

Slowly and painfully she pulled herself up off of the floor and in horror saw a pool of blood where she had lain moments before. She waddled into the bathroom with her jeans around her ankles since James hadn't bothered to pull them off. After cleaning herself up, she went into the kitchen for paper towels and came back to wipe up the mess on the floor.

As she sank to her knees with the wet towels and began the task of cleaning up the blood from her ripped body, the tears came from somewhere deep inside of her and flowed down her face making the pool of redness on the floor more pink, and she scrubbed and scrubbed until the tears stopped, and the floor looked raw.

CHAPTER FOURTEEN

Beverly went back to her normal routine by sheer force of will which sometimes weakened in those darkened moments in the middle of the night. She couldn't escape the fact that James scared her, but she also desperately wanted to please him so he wouldn't be angry with her.

Beverly attended one more group session before the therapist suggested she meet with both the elder Canons.

"I really don't think Beverly needs to come anymore to our group therapy sessions," the therapist began.

"Why not? Is she all right now?" Martha asked. Hollis sat silently by her side.

"Beverly's fine. And she's been fine all along. But let me ask you a question. Why are you so opposed to her dating James?" the therapist asked gently.

"He's no good," Hollis said harshly.

"All right, let's assume that he's no good. By not allowing her to see him, don't you realize that you are making him all the more attractive?" The therapist remained calm.

"What? What kind of nonsense is that?" Hollis demanded.

"No, wait, Hollis. Go on, Doctor," Martha encouraged.

"If you allow Beverly to date James on a fairly limited, somewhat supervised basis, she'll discover on her own what kind of person he is," the therapist suggested.

"But what about our family?" Martha asked.

"What about them? If you raised Beverly as well as I think you did, she'll make wise decisions on her own. But you've also raised her to be independent, so if you restrict her, she'll continue to rebel and maybe not make such wise decisions. Do you remember how it was as a teenager?"

Both Hollis and Martha looked at the therapist as if she'd

94

gone crazy. Hollis began to pace in the small office.

"That's ridiculous! She'll get in trouble!" he yelled.

"She'll get in trouble if you keep her away from him. She's already assured me that she will see James no matter what you say. You may even drive her to a very early marriage and that, no matter how good the intentions, would be trouble." The therapist looked directly at Hollis with a stern expression.

The loud explosive sound came from Hollis' mouth as he finally realized that the therapist probably had earned her money for the day.

"All right, I don't like it, but maybe it's crazy enough to work," Hollis said after a long silence.

And so while Beverly agonized over her situation and the hopelessness of her relationship, she was given permission to begin seeing James openly with certain restrictions.

"You can see him one night a week as long as you are home by ten on school nights or midnight on the weekend. Any other contact will have to be at school or on Sunday during the day," Martha announced that evening after dinner.

Beverly's expression remained grim as her mother delivered the news. Her parents thought she still remained angry with them. In actuality, she felt the bottom drop out from under her again.

James, on the other hand, felt a sense of victory when Beverly delivered the news. He won again, and he had complete control over Beverly. She did whatever he wanted and never really protested. He hardly noticed the change in Beverly. He thought her quietness came from her acceptance of him as the one in charge. He also had plenty of other girls in the wings. Sally wasn't the only one who liked to meet with James after hours. She just had the most accessibility since she stayed home alone most evenings.

James also considered an offer made to him by a local family who had been his most devoted fans during the past basketball season. They knew James suffered a hardship because of the distance to his home and lack of vehicle, and they wanted to help him. Their intentions were sincere but not altogether altruistic. They wanted

some of the attention generated by James. The excitement of winning the state championship had not been erased and high hopes
soared for the coming season and James' last year at VHS. So the
Browns invited James to live with them in Victoria and offered him
the use of their second family car whenever he wanted it. Many
people in town were concerned about James living in Victoria, but
most kept their mouths shut. The Browns had not been raised in
Victoria and did not know about the traditions and neither did they
care.

His mother, understandably, grieved when James told her
because she knew he would have accepted any offer to escape from
Ravens Wood. But she sent him off with a warning. "Once basketball
season ends next year, you will no longer be welcome in that town.
Don't let them get to you, son," she said in a sorrowful way.

"Don't worry, Momma. I've got it all under control. And I'm
going to bring out my girlfriend next Sunday for dinner so make sure
you cook all of your best stuff," James offered as a consolation prize.

And so James began living in town during the spring of 1971
with easy access to Beverly. However, when the Canons heard about
the move, they told Beverly she would no longer be able to baby sit
for the Browns. Even though it galled Beverly when they told her,
they didn't need to worry. One of the conditions for James' living
there required him to babysit when needed. Little did the Browns
know that they left their children with a rapist. Even if they had been
told, they wouldn't have believed it, and like most people of their
generation would have blamed Beverly anyway.

James and Beverly attended Victoria Methodist Church the
following Sunday morning, one of the supervised activities allowed.
When they came into the foyer, the usher who had known Beverly all
her life looked at her with doubtful eyes, and said, "Where do you
want to sit?"

"Up by my mother, Mr. Meyers, just like always."

"There's no room," and he proceeded to direct them to sit in
the very back pew in the farthest corner from the pulpit.

Beverly tried not to notice the slight and hoped James didn't notice the empty spaces next to her mother in the front. No one of any reputation sat in those back pews. They remained reserved for the ushers and bad boys who usually snuck out during the sermon. Certainly no one from Beverly's family had ever sat there. James wasn't completely sure, but he wondered if they had been given these terrible inconspicuous seats because of him.

When he asked Beverly about it on the way to her first visit to Ravens Wood Lake, Beverly denied that any slight had been intended.

"We were just late, that's all, and Mr. Meyers didn't want to take us all the way up front," she told him.

Beverly lied easily because she didn't want a fight on this special day. She hoped that by meeting James' mother, things would improve between them. Even though he didn't believe her, he decided to let it drop for now.

On first entering the community of Ravens Wood Lake, Beverly noticed that all of these homes seemed so much smaller than those in Victoria. She remained unprepared for the shock of seeing James' home for the first time. It was no larger than her living room and dining room combined and the front door was open with no screen door to protect it. She worked hard at hiding her shock, but James sensed her reluctance to enter the house.

"Come on, Beverly, it's time you saw how the other half lives," he remarked sarcastically.

Mrs. Kelly helped her through those first few difficult moments. She embraced Beverly and drew her into the kitchen where the irresistible smells of her Sunday dinner assaulted Beverly's nostrils and brought her back to her senses.

"It's so nice to finally meet you, Mrs. Kelly, and dinner smells wonderful. What are you cooking?"

"Oh, not much, just a pretty simple Sunday dinner. I've got ham in the oven, and I'm about to fry some chicken. There's macaroni and cheese, potato salad, slaw, sweet potato pie, kale, and corn on the cob," she rattled off as she poked around the stove.

"That's so much food! You shouldn't have gone to so much

trouble."

"Honey, that's just a simple Sunday dinner. James told me to just cook my best dishes, and that's what we got."

James and his younger brother began boxing in the living room. Mrs. Kelly just laughed and began teasing them about both being weaklings. Then they both came into the kitchen and starting pulling at her apron, spying into her pots, putting their arms around one another, and calling each other names while laughing.

Beverly had never seen such a loving family. She felt a little better and even envious if this scene indicated how James had been raised. Her family would never be in the kitchen with her mother when she was cooking. But here much loving went into the cooking of this meal. Maybe that's why everything tasted so much better than at her house. She had never even eaten some of the food served that day, but she tried it all and asked how it was all made which endeared her to Mrs. Kelly.

That other girl, Sally, that James sometimes brought home barely spoke to her and never smiled. And they never stayed long enough to eat a meal with the family. Just like Coach Hoover, she would have preferred James to date the girls of Ravens Wood Lake, but he showed little interest in them and they did appear immature next to someone like Beverly. She supposed, as she watched Beverly dig into the kale with gusto, that if he had to date a white girl, it might as well be one as nice and polite as this one. She wondered silently how her parents felt about Beverly's choice in boyfriends.

Some of Beverly's remoteness and distance from James melted that day seeing him in his home environment. She began to feel the old closeness between them return and sensed that he felt the same. She admonished herself for being angry with him. He had endured insult after insult because of her and her family and now, after the incident in church, with the town of Victoria. She decided to come out of her sheltered place and open herself to him once again.

"Why don't we stop somewhere to talk before you take me home, James," Beverly softly spoke into his ear.

He looked at her with a new appreciation. She handled

herself so well in new situations, and his mother really liked her. Now she seemed back to her old self before her family interfered in their life. He pulled off on the next road, and they returned to the feelings that had first attracted them to each other. Beverly came home that afternoon with a flicker of hope that the future might once again be bright.

However, the flicker didn't have a chance to develop into a flame. The next day, James didn't attend school. When Beverly came out into the parking lot after the last bell, James waited in the Brown's car. When she sat in the front seat, he told her he needed to tell her something and knew that she would take the news like a good girl. Instead of going to school, he had visited the doctor in a nearby town because he had been having some problems.

"You see, Beverly, it seems that I've caught gonorrhea somehow, and you've got to go to the doctor yourself and get a shot," he said in one breath.

"What do you mean, 'you caught gonorrhea somehow!'"

"Just what I said. You know things haven't been that great between us lately. I was with another girl a couple of weeks ago, and now we've both got to pay the price. Come on, Beverly, it's not so bad. Everything's different now after yesterday. The doctor is in Chelsea, and he wants to see you tomorrow morning. He doesn't know who you are, but he knows that I could have passed it on to you so he wants to give you a shot so you don't get sick. OK, Bev?" At least he had the decency to be sweet and gentle with her.

The next day, after meeting at school, they drove the fifteen minutes to Chelsea in silence. Beverly's hope had once again been shattered causing her to retreat. James kept trying to talk to her, but she ignored him. She entered the doctor's office embarrassed to even be there but at least thankful that he didn't know her.

When the doctor entered the small room, he told her that they would take a blood test to be sure she didn't carry any other diseases. Then he told her she would receive a shot of penicillin in her buttocks. The nurse would assist. He left the room for a short moment while the nurse helped Beverly pull down her pants. She lay on the cold table on her stomach while the nurse covered her rear in a white sheet. The doctor entered. Luckily she couldn't see the huge needle he carried with a large dose of penicillin. She did feel the shot and cried out slightly in pain.

"Now get dressed, Beverly, and I'll be back in to talk with you," the doctor curtly told her.

When he returned, his face carried a look of sternness.

"Now, James tells me that he wasn't aware you were sleeping with other boys while dating him. You know, you really shook him up when you told him about your symptoms. When he came in to get checked, we did find the bacteria and gave him the necessary treatment. He said that he had only been with you. Now you need to tell all of your other boyfriends, just like you told James so they can also get treatment. And then, Beverly, a nice–looking girl like you should have more respect for herself and stick to one boyfriend at a time."

Beverly stared at him numbly as he turned and walked out of the room. She managed to stumble toward the lobby where a very concerned James led her carefully back to the car.

CHAPTER FIFTEEN

Beverly seethed for the first few miles of the drive back to Victoria. Finally she burst out, "Why did you lie to him?"

"He knew me, and I've got my reputation to protect. One more year here, and then college," he calmly explained.

"How could you? Do you know how embarrassed I was sitting there listening to him lecture me about all of my boyfriends?"

James smirked at that comment which created a fury in Beverly never before surfaced in front of James. She could take just about anything except laughter at her expense especially when she felt so humiliated.

She screamed at him, she ranted, and then she grabbed the wheel of the car in an attempt to get him to pay attention to her. Her hair dampened from her tears formed a ragged mess around her face. At times she was incoherent. James slapped at her a few times to get her to back off but nothing stopped her rage. When she grabbed for the steering wheel, James had had enough. He brought the car under control and pulled off onto the shoulder, methodically put the car in park, and turned and slapped Beverly harder than he ever had. The screaming stopped, but the crying didn't. She continued to sob and mumble to herself until they were on the outskirts of Victoria.

"Who is she?" she demanded.

"Who's who?" he innocently asked.

"You know who, WHO IS SHE?" she screamed.

"No one you would know or need to know about. Mind your own business."

"It is my business, you bastard! She gave me gonorrhea. You better tell me who she is, right now."

By this time, the car had stopped next to the Baptist Church two blocks from Beverly's house. He turned to view her and saw no marks on her face. This time he punched her as hard as a could.

"You don't ever tell me I better do something, do you hear me? I tell you, you don't tell me." This time red marks were visible, but he didn't care; she deserved it.

Beverly huddled next to the door quieted by the blow, not noticing James reaching over her to open the passenger door. He managed to fling it open and gave her a slight shove out the door. She lost her balance and fell on the pavement.

"Get your sorry self home, Beverly. And I hope you learned your lesson," he growled just before slamming the door shut and pulling away from the sidewalk.

She managed to stand up before anyone saw her and quickly walked home. Her parents fortunately were still at work when she came into the house a sniveling, wet mess. When she looked in the mirror the shock numbed her. Her intense crying left red streaks and swollen bags under her eyes and on her right cheek appeared a large red lump swelling before her eyes. She stared for long moments; her scars usually remained hidden inside, but now she wore one on the outside for all to see. Quickly she pulled herself together and went to the freezer for some ice, and then she closeted herself in her bedroom pulling the covers up over her head caressing her cheek with the ice pack.

Beverly truly didn't know what to do next. Slowly as the afternoon ebbed and nightfall came, she knew the first thing would have to be a concoction to explain why she had a swollen cheek. Fortunately, someone in Victoria had died that week so Beverly's parents would be busy with the viewing and comforting of the bereaved. She never imagined herself committing suicide simply because she knew her father would be the one to embalm her. She couldn't stand the thought of his hovering drunkenly over her while he performed the cleansing rituals for the body.

She would tell everyone that in the middle of the night she had woken and walked into the door. Simple, with no details to remember because after all in the concocted story she would have been soundly asleep moments before the lump appeared.

But she still had to face James the next day. Right now she

102

didn't want to ever see him again. That thought came to her slowly as she lay there in her pain. She felt fear when she thought of him. How could she break it off with him without getting killed? Maybe she could just ignore him? He would never stand for that; maybe she would just become so obnoxious that he would break up with her. Who was the other girl or girls he slept with? Maybe she could find out and then threaten them and it would make him so mad, he wouldn't want to see her anymore. All sorts of scenarios played through her head that sleepless night.

Her parents came home around 9:00. She feigned sleep when Martha opened the door a crack to be sure that she was in bed. She made sure to lie on her sore cheek so they couldn't view it until morning.

Sometime during the sleepless night, she realized that she would forgive James. He loved her and without him she had no one to give her attention and take care of her. She vowed to treat him better so he wouldn't have a reason to hurt her.

Beverly played out her story many times the next morning, but with James she didn't need to tell her small lie. He seemed genuinely contrite when he saw her face. He apologized and swore that it would never happen again. He told her that she needed to keep her head about her, too. She just made him so mad that he couldn't control himself. She said little to him and that made him try even harder to be nice to her. Eventually, almost against her will she felt the hardness in her core begin to melt again towards him, and she found herself repeating the promise she had made in the darkened depths of her bedroom the night before. She told him she would work on being a better person. He leaned down and gently kissed her wound, so gently that Beverly didn't even feel his trembling lips as they tried to assuage her pain.

James and Beverly still had certain restrictions on their dating. Somehow her parents felt secure knowing that they had some control over when they saw one another. However, when Connie, Martha's youngest sister called her the next day to see how Beverly was feeling, Martha felt that security slowly ebb.

"What do you mean? Beverly's fine. She just ran into the doorway during the night. Is she in the clinic?"

"I haven't seen Beverly today, Martha, but her name was on the absentee list yesterday," said Connie, a Home Ec teacher at VHS.

"She should have been in school," Martha managed to mumble.

"Then that might explain why James Kelly's name appeared on the list, too," Connie said gently.

Martha slowly hung up the phone. Beverly didn't go to school yesterday and neither did James. Because she had worked at the funeral home all day yesterday, she didn't see Beverly until she got home at 9:00 last night and then she hadn't really seen her; she was asleep in bed which in itself is slightly odd. Beverly usually stayed up past 11:00 even on school nights. And then this morning, Beverly appeared for breakfast with that awful bruise. She had told them something about running into the wall on the way to the bathroom in the middle of the night. Something wasn't quite right. She decided to tell Hollis.

Hollis was at the furniture store this morning trying to work on the books when May stopped by to chat. And May had been doing that quite often in the last few months. He always enjoyed any interruption by May as long as Martha didn't know. Although the visits were innocent enough, somehow he liked to keep them a secret from everyone. So he was glad Martha was at home catching up on some household chores this spring morning.

May had managed to keep her figure through the years and her compensation for marrying a drunken cheat fed her penchant for shopping and nice clothes. Her sandy brown hair still held the same highlights from her youth except now the perfect cut framed her small face. Her body still looked fantastic, and this morning her suit blended perfectly with the contour of her slim body and the low cut neck managed to show the right amount of cleavage which left Hollis just a little breathless when she bent over his desk to give him a quick kiss on the cheek. The two of them made a striking couple, with Hollis' tall frame and distinguished white hair, and May's petite frame.

"Hollis, you work too hard. You should hire someone to take care of all this mundane business. You were probably at the funeral home until late last night, too, weren't you?"

"Well, Steve Cole died this week. There's a viewing every night until the funeral Friday." He couldn't take his eyes off of her as she went to the couch against the wall and sat, crossing her shapely legs and showing some thigh beneath the navy skirt of her suit.

"Still, I worry about you. You need to do something just for yourself sometime. Wouldn't you like that, Hollis?" May asked in her most seductive voice, slowly and deeply.

"Only if you were with me, May," Hollis ventured.

"That could probably be arranged," she replied quietly.

Just then Martha burst into the room so preoccupied that she didn't sense the sexual tension in the air between her husband and sister. Even if she had noticed, Martha's style would not have included confrontation. She hardly remembered anymore that Hollis had been in love with May. Slowly the two pulled their eyes apart from one another and focused on Martha and her distress.

"Connie just called to check on Beverly because neither she nor James attended school yesterday. And then this morning Beverly showed up at breakfast with that swollen cheek," she blurted in one breath.

"Martha, sit down," May commanded as she began to take over the situation.

"What do you think happened, Hollis?" Martha demanded.

Hollis was still trying to recover from his encounter with May. He never shifted gears easily, and it became harder as he grew older.

"I–I'm not sure, but he better not be hurting my little girl. Maybe I'd better talk to him."

"No, Hollis, that's not a good idea," May's tone with him had changed to authority figure rather than seductress. "Let me talk to both of them. Maybe a more objective party can help."

The three decided that May would wait for Beverly at the

Patricia C. Behnke

Canon's house that afternoon while they were at the funeral home. Maybe May could talk some sense into Beverly.

"Aunt May, what's going on?" Beverly inquired when she came home from school that day.

"How did you get that bruise on your cheek?"

"I–I ran into the door. . ."

"Save that for everybody else, Beverly," May interrupted, "but I don't believe it. I'm going to ask again. How did you get that bruise?"

"Obviously you think you already know, Aunt May, so why should I tell you any differently?"

"I know because I live with someone who does the very same thing to me, Beverly. I let him because I don't have a choice, but you do. Get rid of that jerk before it's too late."

May had become hardened before Beverly's eyes. The moment that Beverly felt like breaking down and telling someone the truth passed as May stood tall and unsympathetic before her.

"I expected better from you, Beverly," came the indictment. Then she swept out of the house.

May never talked to James; while she appeared brave and strong in front of her family, she didn't have the nerve to confront someone who disdained women so. She had one of her own to confront every night at home. Hers was a master, however; he would never leave a visible mark. Her minor affairs with other men helped to ease the hurt she felt and allowed her moments to think that maybe she was still attractive. With Hollis, though, she sensed that their recent flirtations might lead somewhere else, and she felt herself careening down a steep precipice toward disaster.

CHAPTER SIXTEEN

May picked up the phone to call her sister wondering how much she should tell her about Beverly. Even though Beverly hadn't said very much, her silence had spoken volumes.

"Martha, she didn't tell me much, but I would keep the two of them apart," she began.

"Did he hit her?"

"I don't know for sure, but she's not a happy girl, and you may just want to put some restrictions on her."

"Thanks, May. I can always count on you. You're the best sister anyone could have."

May managed to gracefully end the phone conversation before the bile rose in her mouth, and she ran to the toilet. She did suffer from a guilty conscience, but she knew herself well enough to know that it wouldn't be enough to keep her from Hollis. After all these years, she slowly realized that she had made a serious mistake in the back seat of that Lincoln so long ago. She loved her son, JJ, but he really was no better at the age of thirty than her husband even though he treated his wife just slightly better. JJ, at least to May's knowledge, didn't hit his wife.

When Beverly's parents came home from the funeral home that evening, they asked her to come out to the living room for a talk.

"Your father and I have decided that you are grounded for the next month for skipping school, and since you skipped school with James, we feel you shouldn't see him either during this time. This includes his coming over here and going to church with you," Martha informed her daughter.

Beverly sat silently and sullenly listening during her mother's pronouncement.

"Is that all?" she finally asked.

"Yes, I think that's it except to say that your father and I are very disappointed in you, Beverly."

Hollis sat stonily listening to his wife and then turned back to the 6:00 news on the TV.

Beverly would never let her parents know it, but in a way, they had unwittingly given her a reprieve from James. Even though he had sweet talked her that morning, she grudgingly admitted to herself that maybe a month away from him might do them both some good.

After Beverly left for her bedroom, Hollis thought about a phone conversation with with his son Tom last week. Tom had asked his father if he knew James Kelly. Cautiously Hollis told him that Beverly and James were friends.

"Why, Tom?" Hollis asked.

"Well, the basketball coach here at the University has been hearing things about James and knew I was from Victoria. He's been asking me to call home to see what I can find out. They're thinking about recruiting him this next year."

"I can mention it to Beverly, Tom. We really don't know him very well."

Now he wondered if maybe encouraging James to talk to this basketball coach from Iowa might not be a bad idea. Iowa's location 500 miles away from Victoria seemed a better distance than a Michigan school which he had heard James was considering. He didn't say anything to Martha; he wanted to think about it some more before he acted.

Later in the evening, Beverly called the Browns' house to talk to James. They told her he had gone out to his mom's for supper.

"Mrs. Kelly? This is Beverly Canon, James' friend?" Beverly said when James' mother answered the phone.

"Well, hello, Beverly. How are you? I just now asked James when he was bringing you out here again. He should've brought you out tonight, sweetie."

"I had tons of homework, but I'd really love to come out again. I had such a good time."

"Oh, I almost forgot. How sweet of you to write me that note

108

thanking me. Nobody's ever done that before," Mrs. Kelly told Beverly.

"Uh, you're welcome, Mrs. Kelly. I'd really like to spend some more time with you." Beverly meant it.

She felt so comfortable in the presence of this kind and warm woman. She imagined climbing right in her lap and telling her all of her troubles. Beverly sensed Mrs. Kelly would understand without judgment.

"Well, I'm sure you didn't call to talk to me, did you? I'll get James. And come out real soon, sugar."

When Beverly told James about her punishment, he said little except that they would have to figure something out. Luckily Sally provided his secret sexual outlet, and he could leave Beverly alone for awhile. Then they'd have to see.

The month passed slowly for Beverly who sat every night at home mostly alone while her parents dealt with one death after another. April seemed to be not only the month of spring's rebirth but a dying month for the old in Victoria. She talked on the phone some with a few friends, mostly Laura who thought Beverly was being mistreated by the whole world. Beverly loved her because she always stood up for her, and Beverly's enemies became her enemies.

It was also Laura who brought the news of James and Sally. James had been bragging to a few of his friends and then last week-end he had taken Sally to some kegger out on state land to what was affectionately called by everyone, "Blueberry Hill." Word spread quickly, of course, as everyone speculated that James and Beverly must have broken up.

Beverly knew Sally and had actually felt sorry for her sometimes. She was quiet and shy and had moved into the area while they were in junior high. Her mother's painful death from cancer had been shared at the Methodist Church where Sally's family had become members. Now evidently not more than a year after her death, Sally's father had been dating a woman in Williamston leaving Sally on her own most of the time. Sally still remained aloof and quiet and kept a shell around her. Maybe that's why Beverly had always thought of her in sympathetic terms because she felt a commonality of spirit between them. But now the news that she might be the one who gave her gonorrhea changed Beverly's opinion and left her despising Sally.

She decided not to say anything to James, but to just watch what happened in the hallways at school. Now that she had an enemy, James became worth defending.

Hollis decided to first broach the subject of James and Iowa State to May. She always reasoned things through before making a decision, he rationalized as he dialed her number the next afternoon. But why did his hand shake as his finger sought out the correct hole for dialing? Why did he take a sharp intake of breath when she answered the phone with her sensual, "Hello?"

"May, this is Hollis. I was wondering if we could talk today. Alone."

"Of course, Hollis. Where?"

"It's quiet down here at the store, and Martha's gone into Ann Arbor for her big grocery shopping so we probably wouldn't be interrupted."

"That would be fine, Hollis," she said barely above a whisper.

When she entered the office, Hollis locked the door behind her so the clerk couldn't enter without knocking first. He brushed past her and could smell the faint traces of Chanel above her own sweet aroma. He turned back around and saw that she hadn't moved. He turned toward her. They embraced, and Hollis could feel the sensation of her ample breasts press against his chest. He began rubbing her back as they pressed closer together. She could feel all parts of him come to life. For a brief moment, it seemed as if they were trying to melt into one another before coming to their senses.

Unwillingly, they pulled apart and uncomfortably went to their positions, his behind the desk, hers in front. They both felt dizzy and extremely aroused from that brief encounter. They usually hugged when they saw one another, brotherly/sisterly hugs. But this was different. They had embraced as lovers, and the flush on each of their faces would have given them away if anyone had walked into the room at this moment. It took them both a few moments to recover and begin talking about the topic at hand.

"Tom called last week. He said the coach at Iowa is interested in James Kelly. Tell me, you've talked to Beverly, will she continue with James even though we forbid it?"

"I'm afraid so, Hollis. I think he's got her under his spell. I should know. She's got all the signs of a female who can't break away."

"Damn! Why with him? He'll bring her nothing but heartache, and their life together would be hell. Beverly just doesn't see these things. It's not that I'm prejudiced at all; it's just the way things are. It's not the kind of life I want for her."

"What about Iowa?"

"Well, I wondered, if Beverly really had her heart set on James, what would happen if he was 500 miles away playing basketball during her senior year of high school? Wouldn't there be a good chance that Beverly would maybe lose interest?"

"Not a bad idea, Hollis. Time is different when you are that age. A month can seem like a year and nine months might give a girl a chance to learn some independence. It's not like that now with us, is it, Hollis?"

"May, I. . ."

"It's OK, I only meant, I could wait a long time for something to happen between us, and I wouldn't lose interest at this stage in my life. It was different when I was a teenager." May spoke very softly and apologetically refusing to lift her eyes to those of Hollis now boring holes into her.

"Thank you for saying that, May. It means everything to me." Hollis reluctantly turned his eyes to the papers in front of him. "I guess I'll talk to Martha next. She should be in on the plan, too."

May left quickly before anything more could happen between them. And they both knew that something more would happen.

On her way out the door, she passed Karen just coming into

work. But Karen seemed distracted and didn't even acknowledge May as she walked past her to the closet where the brooms were kept.

"Karen, aren't you late today?" Hollis asked as he came out of the office to admire May's retreating figure.

"Oh, I'm sorry, Mr. Canon, it won't happen again. Coach needed me to stay after school today," Karen said with her head bent over the broom.

"That's OK, I just wanted to make sure you were all right. Listen, can you dust the end tables today after you finish sweeping?"

"Sure, I'll get right on it."

Karen worked quickly and efficiently, but her mind wasn't on her work. She kept remembering the way Bill Hoover had come up behind her while she filed some papers this afternoon. He just stood there pressing harder and harder against her back side until she couldn't take it any more. She turned around to him and slowly unbuttoned her short culotte dress. He began caressing her breasts as he pulled them out of the bra cups. He then began to press against the front of her until she had sunk to the floor and helped him relieve himself of all that pressure of being a big time state championship coach.

CHAPTER SEVENTEEN

"Martha, I've been thinking. You know Bev will probably continue seeing James no matter what we say."

"What makes you say that?"

"Well, I talked to May yesterday, and she thinks that Beverly probably can't stay away, particularly if we forbid it." Hollis hesitated bringing May into the picture but decided he needed some backup in order to present his radical solution.

"You talked to May about Bev? When?"

"She stopped by the store to look at the bedroom suite she's been thinking about buying, and I asked her what she thought." He hurried through this part so his wife wouldn't wonder why he asked May before her. "I keep remembering the phone call from Tom last week, asking about James Kelly."

"You didn't tell me about that, Hollis."

"I guess at the time it didn't seem important. Tom asked if we knew James because the basketball coach at Iowa has been showing interest in recruiting him."

"What's that got to do with us or Bev?"

"Well, if James goes to a college so far away, won't it be difficult for him to continue influencing Beverly so strongly?"

Martha stopped to think for a moment, and even though it seemed to reek of duplicity, she had to agree that Hollis made sense. She wanted more than anything to be rid of James Kelly forever. Everywhere she went, Martha felt the town gossiping about her daughter and James.

"What do we do, dear?"

"First, when her grounding is up at the end of the month, we allow them to see each other again, on a limited basis stressing that we won't tolerate skipping school. Then as his senior year progresses, we quietly do what we can to help Tom and the Iowa coach lure James away."

"You've thought this thing through, haven't you?" Martha desperately hoped her husband knew what they might be forced to do.

"Yes, and I don't see another solution. It may even make our lives livable for the next year."

"I just want Beverly to stop seeing him. But you may be right, Hollis. I'll do whatever you want."

Hollis looked at his wife with an appreciative eye. He had been aroused since yesterday in the office with May. He needed an outlet even if it wasn't with May. His wife could help release some of the pressure. He approached Martha from behind as she washed the dinner dishes.

"How about putting this all down, Martha, and forgetting about everything for awhile?" He began rubbing against her and kissing her neck.

"Hollis, stop that! I've got to finish the dishes and Beverly will be home from Youth Group soon. What's gotten into you?" She turned around slightly and gave her husband a chastising look.

"Nothing, Martha." He shook his head dejectedly and sighed. "I'm going down to the funeral home for a little while. Don't wait up for me." Hollis grabbed his jacket and headed out the door leaving his wife with a puzzled look on her face.

Hollis parked outside the basement door and went down the stairs into his work room. The embalming room always looked clean but still smelled of formaldehyde no matter what. The metal table glistened in the glare of the lights hung above it. Hollis moved it slightly to hide the drain in the floor beneath it. He then opened one of the cabinet doors at the end of the table and found his supply of whiskey. Pouring himself a shot, he leaned against the table and thought about May.

May also thought of Hollis that night. Her husband, Johnny, of course, had left after an argument at dinner, and May felt restless in the big empty house. She decided to take a drive to clear her head of the lustful scenes which hadn't left her mind since her embrace

114

A Victorian Justice

with Hollis yesterday.

When she passed the funeral home, she noticed the lights on in the basement but nowhere else on the premises. That was strange because if someone had died usually the lights were on all over the home. She drove up to the side door leading to the basement stairs and noticed that it was open. Curious, she parked and entered, taking the steps quietly down into the basement. The door to the embalming room itself was open, and she could see Hollis with a shot glass in his hand, leaning on the table deep in thought.

"Hollis, are you OK?"

He looked up startled to hear the voice he had just been imagining. "May, come in. Have a drink."

"Thanks. What are you doing here? Are you waiting for a body to be delivered?" She knew that the embalming needed to be performed within eight hours of death so it would not be unusual for him to be waiting for a corpse so he could begin right away.

"No, nothing like that. I just felt a little at loose ends tonight, and I came here to think."

"Me, too. I mean, I felt a little at loose ends, too and decided to take a drive. Johnny got mad at me again tonight because he didn't like the way I cooked his steak so he left in a hurry after dinner."

"Aaah, May, he's a fool," Hollis whispered and gulped the rest of his drink before refilling the glass.

"What about you, Hollis?"

"Don't ask, May. I don't want to talk about your sister."

Silence fell between them as they each sipped their drinks. Then Hollis poured some more. Soon they both lost some of their inhibitions and began the age–old art of flirting shamelessly with one another.

"Do you remember when we used to sit in my Model A and dream about the future, May?"

"I don't remember us talking very much at all." She came close to him and rested her head against his shoulder. Hollis pulled her closer and began saying her name over and over again.

The passion that they both had been feeling for the past few

115

months erupted into an immediate volcano of action as they sought each others' lips pressing their bodies closer and closer together. Hollis clumsily unbuttoned May's blouse exposing her luscious breasts concealed only by the black chemise worn beneath. He then found the zipper on the back of her skirt and pulled it down around her ankles leaving her practically naked before him. He took a great intake of breath. He had never seen such loveliness.

"May, you are so beautiful. Why did I ever let you go?" he breathed in her ear as she began undoing his buttons, pulling off his shirt and then undershirt, reaching for the belt of his pants, finding the zipper and leaving him exposed to her for the first time.

Hollis released himself from her grasp and fumbled around for an old blanket kept in one of the cupboards. He covered the cold, steel table. He tenderly turned to May and easily picked her up and set her down on the table. But before lying down, she pulled off her chemise and bra exposing herself to the coolness of the room and to her lover. Hollis moaned and joined her on the table, and there in the loneliness of the death room, they learned the secrets of each other kept hidden for the past thirty years.

In their passion, both had forgotten that the door had been left open to the basement. Beverly, on her way home from church, wondered why May's car was parked there with the lights on in the basement. Probably May and her mother were doing something down there, she thought. She went home without bothering to stop.

One person who did bother to stop on his way home was Johnny Randall. He saw his wife's car and pulled up next to it. He saw the open door and entered. The couple on the table were so engrossed in their lovemaking and making so much noise, that they didn't hear him as he walked down the steps, and they didn't see him stand in the doorway for a split second before bolting back up the stairs. They didn't even hear the slamming of the car door before Johnny tore out of the parking lot.

Luckily for May, he had been drinking heavily and drank some more before she gathered herself together to go home. By the time she entered their darkened house, he had passed out on the

116

living room floor.

Beverly had forgotten about May's car by the time she came into the house so her mother's presence in front of the TV didn't really surprise her. She told her mother good night and went into her room.

Hollis couldn't go home that night, but Martha was used to his habits by now. It didn't seem a bit unusual that he had left the house slightly agitated and then didn't return until morning. She didn't allow drinking in the house, but she could always tell when he needed the release bestowed upon him by his whiskey. She didn't approve, but it was easier than having him paw her all night.

When Hollis woke the next morning on the cool steel table covered in the blanket still carrying May's scent, he felt better than he had in years. Stronger and more capable of facing the day's activities, he rose and went to the small sink to wash his face. He heard a knock on the side door and with a little regret went to see who might be there. It was Martha.

"Hollis, Joan Feeley just called. Her father, Rex passed away early this morning. The family wants you to handle everything," Martha announced when he opened the door.

"OK, where is the body?"

"The ambulance from the hospital is transporting it right now."

"Thanks, Martha. You can tell the family that I'll be ready to see them around 1:00 p.m. and make sure George can handle everything at the furniture store. I don't think anything major is happening this week." He turned around and left her standing there on the stoop.

She walked away wondering what change had come over Hollis. Seldom did he handle all of the details of death so efficiently. And giving her orders! She usually just dealt with everything without consulting him. She wondered when he would be ready for retirement. It was a grueling business. None of his sons wanted anything to do with the funeral home although, thankfully, George helped with little things like driving the hearse or limo for the funerals, and he would come down and be in attendance when needed during visitations, but he wanted nothing to do with the preparing and preserving of the body. However, he practically managed the furniture store now even though Hollis still insisted on keeping hours there and overseeing the books. Sometimes she wondered if George resented it. She sighed as she thought about Hollis having to sell the funeral home and wondered if he would be able to let it go even though he acted as if he disdained the whole business.

When the late Rex Feeley was delivered to him that morning, Hollis set about his business without taking even one sip. He washed him carefully and thought about Rex and remembered fondly all their escapades as young boys on the dirt roads and in the trees of Victoria. Rex had died of cancer, and he looked very tired. Hollis knew though that he could give him the appearance of peaceful repose as if he hovered between the sleeping and the dead. Many families complimented him on his handiwork, and he felt a special compunction to give Rex back some of the dignity lost during his ugly struggle with cancer.

When Joan, her mother, and her brother entered the funeral home office that afternoon, they all hugged Hollis and thanked him for taking care of the all the details.

"Hollis, Dad became very concerned at the end about people seeing him bald, and he requested that we have a closed casket," Joan announced almost immediately.

"But, Joan, people need to see him. You saw him die; others need to see him so they can begin the mourning and healing process. Your father had many friends in this town."

"Yes, we know, but Dad requested this."

"You haven't seen what I can do, Joan. He'll just look like he's passing into another stage, a peaceful stage."

Rex's wife, Nancy, remained quiet as did the son. They all looked to Joan, the unmarried matriarch of the family to handle this situation.

"I'm not sure, Hollis. It's not what he wanted."

"Sometimes we have to go ahead and do what's best for the

118

living rather than the dead. I have a suggestion. Why don't you wait and see how nice your father looks and then the family can have a private viewing tomorrow before we open the doors for the public visitation. You can decide then if you want it open or closed."

"OK, that sounds reasonable." And all three grieving family members acquiesced to his demands.

"Now, let's go up and choose the proper casket for burying your dear father and husband." As Hollis led the way upstairs, the family followed not knowing what traps lay ahead.

CHAPTER EIGHTEEN

Coach Bill Hoover tried to enjoy his extra freedom now that basketball season had ended so successfully. At the very end of the season, the Detroit News named him 1971 "Coach of the Year" for the entire state. VHS Principal Joe Meyer, quoted in the article which announced Bill's new honor, said, "Bill has tremendous ability to work with young people because he cares so much about them."

Once all this excitement abated, Coach spent some time cruising the roads at Ravens Wood Lake because he knew he needed someone to replace James after the next season. He watched James' younger brother, Joshua, very carefully but so far at thirteen he didn't display the same agility of his older brother. But he was still growing and coming out of his awkward stage. No one else seemed very promising as yet either.

He would spend time talking to Joshua and his friends as they all crowded around his brand new Mustang convertible which he had purchased soon after the state championship as a reward to himself.

"Can you take us for a drive?" they would all clamor.

Wanting to remain on good terms with these young potential players, he always opened the door on the passenger side, and they would all climb in, five and six at a time. He'd take them around the tiny community so everyone could see them, and then he'd go out on the main road and give them a thrill at some higher speeds.

"Come on, Coach, just one more time around the block," one of the boys always yelled as they pulled back onto the dirt roads of Ravens Wood.

"Can't today, boys, but you guys keep playing basketball. I'm going to make one of you a star."

They'd all look at him with wide grins and offer assurances that they would keep practicing. One of them would always ask if he was coming out next weekend.

On this Saturday, he waved to Mrs. Kelly who stood in the doorway of her small home.

"Coach, now you come on in here for some lunch. I've got plenty," she yelled.

"I'm sure you do, but I can't today. Got to get back to my little woman, you know. She'd be jealous if she knew I ate lunch with another woman."

Mrs. Kelly waved both hands at him with a smile, but she knew better. He wasn't eating lunch with them today because he didn't have any persuading to do yet with one of the young boys.

He enjoyed these visits most of the time, but on this particular day in May he felt uneasy. James had been fairly uncommunicative to him lately, and that worried him. Was another high school spending time recruiting him? While it was not considered gentlemanly to do so, it sometimes happened especially with someone of James' capabilities. He thought that if the situation reversed itself, he would probably consider recruiting James, too. Well, he'd have James come out to his lake place this summer and let him use the boat, bring a girl, meet his wife and just generally get James to relax around him. They had one more season to go and could win state again.

Bill Hoover's wife also seemed a little distant lately. He loved Alice and had known her since they both began college in 1960, although she didn't excite him any more. But he was good to her, and his little escapades didn't have any impact on how he felt about her. However, he worried now that she might have heard something. He'd just have to face that problem in the way he usually did. Alice loved him without reservation and believed everything he told her if he did it with roses, jewelry, or wine. During college he'd even been caught literally with his pants down once or twice. But Alice always bought his lame stories if he just handled her correctly. Her father hadn't been much different from Bill so she did the same as her mother had done for years. She looked the other way.

But Bill couldn't afford to take chances. Without Alice's

121

family money, they wouldn't enjoy the lifestyle to which he had become accustomed. He was the only teacher he knew with two homes and a new car every year, and he enjoyed it. He needed Alice.

Karen also presented a problem. She would graduate next month and go away to college in the fall. Soon he would gently end their affair. But she began showing signs of wanting more from him. She became jealous when he couldn't see her, and she mentioned his wife's name far too often for his tastes. In fact, he never wanted his wife's name mentioned by any of his girls.

However, Karen still excited him with her big dark eyes and abundant hair and breasts. Now that the weather had warmed up she wore mini skirts and shorts and halter tops which kept him in a perpetual state of arousal when in her presence. This excitement worried him. He never let himself get emotionally involved with his dalliances, but Karen kept persisting in teasing him just by her very existence. His emotions always seemed on edge in her presence. And now, on the weekend, he could think of nothing but her. He'd even pushed her to have sex with him in the office after school last week while the secretaries were still there. He had broken one of his cardinal rules which he had set for himself when he began teaching.

Just thinking about her on this beautiful spring morning made him want her in the most desperate way. He stopped at the gas station a few miles from Ravens Wood and called her house. Luckily she answered the phone so he didn't have to hang up.

"Can you meet me somewhere?" he demanded without preamble.

"I've got to go down to the furniture store and work this afternoon. They need extra help in the showroom because of a funeral."

"What time?"

"Well, I need to be there in two hours."

"Meet me outside my back office door in twenty minutes," he said before abruptly hanging up.

Karen smiled to herself. She knew she had him now. Calling on a Saturday, a day reserved solely for his wife. But he had called her instead. She also smiled because a month earlier she had stopped taking the pill which Bill had insisted she take. She didn't like the way it had changed her body, and besides she was ready to play for keeps.

Exactly twenty minutes later he pulled up outside of the office door and saw Karen walking down the alley toward him. She looked very demure in her white blouse and brown mini–skirt. He went into the office and left the door open a crack. As Karen approached the door, she looked around to make sure no one saw her, and then she entered the darkened office shutting and locking the door behind her.

He barely gave her time to adjust to the low lighting from the harsh sunlight outside when he was upon her. She told him to slow down.

"Come on, Bill. Don't rip my blouse," she said softly as she rubbed up against him.

"Then take the damn thing off, now," he pleaded, his voice rising in high–pitched desperation.

She unbuttoned the blouse slowly and carefully watching his face as beads of perspiration appeared on his forehead. She pulled off her blou`se revealing her white lace 38C bra overflowing with young pink flesh. He grabbed both breasts and practically lifted them out of their cups before she could unsnap the back strap.

Then they both sank to the floor of the office where Bill Hoover had lectured James Kelly about high school girls who could bring him down.

Later Karen walked cheerfully to the furniture store on Main Street. George Canon greeted her as she entered the front door.

"Oh, Karen, I'm glad you're a few minutes early. I just called your house, but your mom said you had left an hour ago. I've got to drive the hearse for a two o'clock funeral so I just need you to hold down the fort. You know we get a lot of browsers on Saturday."

"No problem, Mr. Canon. Do you want me to lock up at five o'clock?"

"I should be back by four so that won't be necessary. When

123

there aren't any customers maybe you could dust and sweep a little today, too."

"Sure thing, see you around four," and Karen went to work humming and smiling to herself.

Bill Hoover stayed in his office long minutes after Karen had left. What was it about that girl? And today he had made a fatal mistake. He had shown her that he needed and wanted her almost desperately, and he knew she had been astute enough to understand that. He saw it in her eyes and her tone as she treated him as a young child too eager on a Christmas morning. He would have to stay away from her for awhile. Maybe he would just allow himself one last fling before she left for college in early September. Even as he made this vow to himself he remembered how she looked as she unbuttoned her blouse, and he knew he couldn't keep this promise. He felt himself addicted to this young girl's body, and he was at the mercy of his lust for more of it.

He pulled himself up from behind the desk, ran his fingers over his crew cut and tucked in his knit shirt. Outside in the daylight, he shook the demons from his head before getting behind the wheel of his beautiful convertible when he remembered what was at stake with Karen. Then he drove home to Alice who he knew waited patiently for his return.

CHAPTER NINETEEN

Spring brings renewal and leads directly into the fresh mowed aroma that makes up a Michigan summer. Lilacs bloom on over–sized bushes in the yards giving off the sweet perfume smell of spring time. The richness of this season comes from the long hibernation of all growing things during the long winter months in this frozen northern climate. When finally the folks can get out and enjoy the signs of the season, much socializing begins, starting with the remembrance of the country's war dead.

The Memorial Day weekend marked the official season opening for summer and marked the first day that any socially prominent Victorian woman could officially wear white shoes to church.

Memorial Day began at the high school with bands and veterans leading the way to the town's cemetery. Hollis always prayed that no one died during this weekend because so much of the holiday centered around the twenty–one gun salute in the middle of the cemetery honoring all of the town's war heroes. He tried to avoid a funeral on this day at all costs. The day ended where it began with the American Legion members passing out free ice cream bars to all in attendance. For the Stuart and Canon families, the tradition continued with a picnic lunch in Grandma Stuart's backyard with barbecued chicken and potato salad.

The previous week Beverly's grounding had been lifted. Her parents sat her down and gravely informed her that they had done a lot of thinking during the past month.

"Are you still determined to see James?" Martha asked tentatively.

"Yes," came the sullen reply.

"Then your father and I agree that it would be hopeless to try and prevent you from seeing him. You may date him on a limited basis. I think one night a week for starters would be appropriate."

"I agree with your mother, Beverly."

While James seemed pleased with the news, when she tried to invite him to the annual Memorial Day picnic, he just snorted and said, "No, thank you." So Beverly went alone with her parents to her grandmother's house.

For the past few weeks Johnny Randall had been acting very strangely although only May noticed the subtle change. He stayed home more and drank less. Something kept nagging at the back of his mind as if he should remember something quite important. He began noticing May more and watching her more suspiciously. Somehow he imagined that the thing he couldn't remember had something to do with his wife.

It worried May. She kept telling herself that she was paranoid. She felt guilty about her tryst with Hollis, adultery which bordered on incest because of the close family relationship involved. Johnny never noticed anything about her, she thought. He had probably just gotten dumped by his latest conquest and so he hung around the house more, she told herself in her worst moments.

She and Hollis had managed to avoid one another for the past three weeks except for inescapable meetings at church and on the street of the small town. But she stayed away from the furniture store and the funeral home. She knew if she was alone with Hollis it would happen all over again and while every fiber of her being longed for that, she knew she had to put a brake on the emotional roller coaster ride for now.

Hollis had a busy month and on the surface barely noticed May's absence. He just felt a warm glow whenever he thought of her, and he had no desire to be with his wife intimately during this time. He didn't know if history would repeat itself, but he had little time to think about it or even analyze it. Ever since Rex Feeley's death, he'd had one funeral after another. One week he'd even had to deal with two funerals.

As he prepared for the day's events, he looked forward to relaxing. Thank goodness no one rested at the Canon Funeral Home today. He could enjoy the family and gaze upon May. That's really all he asked for in life. Anything else became a bonus.

By the time everyone headed up to Grandma Stuart's house, the day had warmed and the thunder clouds of the morning had disappeared after their few attempts at rain. Hollis, Martha, and Beverly arrived at the same time as George and his family and spent a good half an hour greeting all of the extended family gathered for the day.

As usual May and Johnny arrived late. Even JJ and his wife had managed to be there on time. Johnny didn't look drunk today, but sometimes it became difficult to judge early in the day. Besides he always brought his silver flask to these events, and no one knew when he might emerge from the bathroom in a rage. May looked breathtaking in her halter top dress with full skirt and high heels. She always managed to capture the perfect look showing just the right amount of cleavage and shoulder without looking cheap. No one could compete with her for style, and no one tried. At one time her sisters resented her for it, but now they all knew what a difficult life she led with Johnny, and everyone in the family judged her as a saint for sticking with him for all of these years. Rumors of her own affairs had abated in the last decade and were forgotten.

"May, you look beautiful! Now I know where you've been all month. You've been out buying the prettiest dress possible for today," Martha, dressed in a plain house dress, gushed as she embraced her older sister.

"You look good, too, Martha," May lied.

Hollis stood just behind Martha waiting to greet his sister–in–law. He didn't know if he had the strength to simply lean down and give her a quick peck on the cheek. He really just wanted to undo the strings of her halter which tied at the back of her neck.

"Hello, Hollis. I see that you've been pretty busy this month. It's good to see you."

"May, you do look lovely today," he mumbled as he leaned down slightly and managed to barely kiss the air near her cheek before turning abruptly away and heading for the bathroom.

Hollis and May managed to avoid one another for most of the party. However, once they both ended up at the buffet table together with no one else, and Hollis asked quietly how she was.

"I miss you, Hollis, but I thought it best to stay away for awhile."

"It's hard to know what to do, isn't it? I've had a difficult month, but in the back of my mind always remained the image of you," Hollis managed to whisper as he leaned down to grab a cup of punch.

"Maybe we can work something out soon."

"I hope so, May."

Johnny Randall watched the two of them through the screen of the back porch and wondered why they were standing so close and talking in such low tones. He glared at them and felt the fog lift for a moment, but then nothing. He shrugged and headed for the bathroom and his silver flask which he hadn't touched all day.

Karen stared listlessly at the ceiling of her bedroom and wondered what had happened. Ever since that Saturday three weeks ago, Bill had studiously avoided her and hadn't even asked her to work late one single night. She had thought that things were going to change now after seeing that look in his eyes, but he didn't seem very interested anymore. On top of that her period started last week and so she had no trump card at all to play. She never really wanted to go to college but when she was offered the scholarship last fall, she knew she would accept. However, she'd rather be married to Bill Hoover so she could get away from her family who she very rarely saw anyway. When her parents weren't working, they spent long hours in the bars from Victoria to Dexter spending most of their overtime money on cheap beer and cigarettes.

There remained one week of school, and she began to plot and devise ways that she could again see that needy and hungry look manifest itself within Bill's eyes. She knew she could do it, and she knew how. By seventeen, Karen had learned very quickly that the way into a man's heart and pants centered around the very ample charms above her waist, and she planned to use them in her attack.

Bill Hoover had made a decision three weeks ago as he drove his Mustang home to his wife. He would not have anything to do with Karen until school let out for the summer. It was too dangerous because he wanted her constantly. If he didn't exert some self–control, they were going to get caught. And that he couldn't allow because he wanted his lifestyle to remain intact, and he definitely wanted another state championship. Once his wife had moved out to the lake place after Memorial weekend, he would breath easier about Karen. They could even use his house in Victoria if they were careful. It certainly would be safer than either his car or office at school.

James called Beverly that night after the picnic, and they talked for a long time.

"How'd it go today with all those Canons and Stuarts gathered in one place?" he asked almost sweetly.

"I missed you."

"Well, maybe next time. I just don't think your family's ready for me yet. Listen, I've been meaning to tell you, I'm leaving for basketball camp next week after school ends."

"How come you didn't tell me?"

"I just found out for sure, and we haven't really had a whole lot of time to talk lately, have we? Anyway, it's at Houghton Lake for a month. This is a great opportunity for me, Bev. The camp is being run by U of M coaches and players so I'll be working with the best basketball people in the state."

"That's good, James, but a month! Don't you get to come home at all?"

"Once after two weeks. We'll make up for lost time then, baby. Hey, listen to this. Coach Hoover's invited us out to his lake place this summer to swim and ski. He said he and his wife had been waiting to invite us after they had moved out there for the summer. How about it?"

"God, I can't believe it, that scum! When do we go?"

"Hah, that's the spirit, girl. We'll go and have a good ole time watching him play hubby and trying to get on my good side."

129

They both chuckled.

"I do feel sorry for her, though, James."

"Well, she shoulda known better than to marry him."

CHAPTER TWENTY

The school year ended, and summer began in earnest in Victoria. Cloudless days and starry nights created a sense of security at least until August when the weather became cooler and hints of winter could be felt in the air. But June and July brought fresh raspberries from wild bushes as well as rhubarb which sweetened just right made a heavenly pie. The sod farmers worked overtime and residents in Victoria hoped the winds remained calm because the muck fields which held the sod until it was removed blew loose black dirt into the town when a storm brewed and window ledges carried the black silt until fastidious housewives came to wipe it away.

James left for his basketball camp, and Beverly settled into the summer routine of sleeping late and babysitting George's two sons whenever Susan had to work. Susan also helped out during the funerals. Beverly's family kept her out of the business side of things for the most part. Martha Canon didn't think it was proper for her to work in the store when the Canons could afford to hire someone like Karen who needed the money more.

Karen had worked very hard on Coach during the last week of school and finally he capitulated on the last day after everyone had departed in a frenzy of water balloons and squirt guns. He had tried so hard to avoid her and ignore her, but on this day she looked so beautiful and sweet. Yet her tight T– shirt and short shorts gave her sensual nature away. When she came close to him as he sat at his desk finishing up his grades, he felt her breasts brush up against his neck, and he could no longer keep his vow to himself. He pulled her down on top of him and barely managed to pull down her shorts before roughly completing the act. She even managed to get him excited again, and this time they slowed their frenzied pace as she performed some basic rituals which left him only wanting more of

131

her.

Karen was certain she would hear from him some more this summer. Bill was certain, too.

May and Hollis managed to stay away from one another for about a month after their first encounter. Then one night May visited the basement again leaving her car at home and walking through the darkened streets of Victoria to her lover, her sister's husband. They locked the door and did not bother to have a drink before running to one another's arms.

Hollis held her close for a long moment, and the only sounds came from the two hearts beating in unison. He pushed her away slightly so he could look into her face.

"God, May, I've missed you. You smell so good," Hollis croaked when he could find his voice.

May smiled and took him by the hand. She knew he kept a cot in the back room where he could sleep on those nights he didn't make it home. Sometimes he never made it off the embalming table even though the cot remained made up and ready for his drunken body. They sat down together and spent a long time just holding one another. Finally they helped each other undress slowly savoring each moment like a fine wine. When Hollis finally entered her, they looked at one another without moving. Both of their eyes filled with tears as they realized this act made them complete. When they were finished, they lay for a long time talking about their lives and hopes and dreams. Neither had ever had moments like this one during their respective marriages.

When James came home for his weekend break mid–way through the camp, he asked Beverly to go to the Coach's lake house with him. She reluctantly said yes although she really didn't want to sit around with Mrs. Hoover and pretend that she had a loving husband.

When they arrived, the Hoovers greeted James and Beverly and offered them soft drinks. Alice Hoover set about at once to make them feel comfortable and welcome in their simple summer cottage.

"What are you doing this summer, Beverly?" she sweetly

asked.

"I'm babysitting some, but really not much."

"You don't help out down at the furniture store or funeral home?"

Thinking of Karen sweeping the floors and sneaking out of Coach's back door, Beverly hesitated, "Uh, no, my mom and dad don't think it's a good idea that I should work when there are other girls who need the money more."

"Oh, who's working for them this summer? I knew the girl who worked there this past year, I think. Karen, was her name?"

"Y–yes, she's working there," Beverly answered nervously.

"Yes, Karen worked for Bill this past year, too. Nice girl."

"What are you girls talking about?" Bill asked as he and James entered the room with soft drinks.

"I was asking Beverly about Karen. You know, your office aide this past year. She works for Hollis and George down at the store."

"Karen might have mentioned that. She's a hard worker, that's for sure. I'll have a hard time replacing her next year," Bill said smoothly before changing the subject to boats and skiing.

James and Beverly caught one another's eyes and tried not to smile.

"James, how's camp? I've heard some good reports on you."

"I'm learning a lot, Coach, but it's hard work. I'm sore all of the time. I've never been challenged like that on the court."

"Well, maybe there's hope for state again this year, huh?"

"I hope so, since I'm sure there'll be lots of recruiters at those games."

"Now, James, be careful with them. They might offer you all sorts of things, but don't let your head be turned. Go for the best, most solid offer. I can help you sort some of it out if you want."

"Well, yeah, I've got a lot to consider, I guess."

"By the way, there's a tournament in Indiana in October for All Star players from the Midwest. I can probably get the school to sponsor you, if you're interested. There's usually a lot of scouts at these things, so it would be a great opportunity. You'll start making college decisions a few months after that."

"Sounds good, Coach."

James and Beverly spent the rest of the day enjoying the lake by boating and swimming. They even began to feel comfortable with the Hoovers. Beverly managed to stop thinking about Karen, and James relaxed. James went back to basketball camp content and happy with his life.

Actually James and Beverly ended up having a nice summer with only one incident to put an ugly mark on their first one together.

The weekend that camp ended, James came home on Saturday. Beverly hadn't heard from him by early evening so she decided to go to a grasser with her friends, Laura and Mary. Grassers are not so unique to teenagers eager to find ways to spend those long Michigan summer nights, and the ones around Victoria contained all the ingredients necessary to an evening of drinking and partying out of sight of any nosy adult.

Beverly had been spending quite a bit of time at home since March, and this really was her first party in a long time. She looked forward to laughing and relaxing with some old friends from school. She had forgiven many of them and even made some new friends this past year despite James' hold on her.

They began drinking on the way to the party by opening a bottle of Boone's Farm Strawberry Hill. It only cost a dollar and could be shared by three or four people. By the time Beverly arrived, the bottle was gone, and she was on her way.

She wandered over to the fire just getting started and noticed Sally standing there. Beverly hadn't spoken to her since she found out about her and James, and her presence at this party seemed slightly out of place.

Beverly glared at her for a long moment. Sally glanced up at her looking through the lens of her thick brown glasses. Sally immediately broke eye contact and looked into the fire. Beverly sauntered over to where Sally stood.

"So how are you tonight, Sally?"

No answer. Sally wanted to run but her legs wouldn't carry her. Beverly must have found out somehow.

"I asked you how you were. How come you can't answer me?"

"Lay off her, Bev," said one of the boys standing around the fire.

"Me, lay off her? That's funny. If she'd stop laying with all the guys around here, maybe everyone would be a lot healthier."

"Come on, Bev, let's go back to the car," urged Mary.

"Just a minute. Listen, Sally, stay away from James, do you hear me? I'll beat the shit out of you if I hear anything about you, or if I ever catch anything again." Mary managed to pull Beverly away just as she leaned down into Sally's face creating a very threatening stance.

Sally went over to a large rock on the outskirts of the main party as the tears roll down her cheeks. She made no sound, but when James arrived shortly afterwards, he saw her sitting all alone looking sad and damp.

"What happened, Sally?"

"Beverly."

"What about Beverly? Is she here?"

She nodded her head. "She knows," came the dull response.

"What did she say?"

"She threatened me to stay away from you, and she mentioned the clap."

James who had no great feeling one way or another for Sally knew she didn't deserve to be humiliated in front of everyone by Beverly. Also, why hadn't Beverly waited at home for him to call and say he had returned?

"Where is she?"

Sally pointed her head in the direction of Mary's car. James slowly stood and patted Sally on the back. Then he walked over to the car and opened the back door and stepped in.

"James, when did you get here?" Beverly asked from the front seat where she sat drinking beer with Mary.

135

"Just now. What are you doing here? Why didn't you wait until I called before coming out here?"

Mary snickered in the front seat but said nothing.

"I said, what are you doing here?"

"I'm partying. What are you doing here? Did you come to meet Sally? If so, she's sitting on that rock over there waiting." Beverly had begun to get angry at his tone.

James reached up and grabbed her hair and pulled her head back to the headrest in the front seat.

"Leave Sally out of this. Why'd you start messing with her anyway?" He pulled tighter.

"Let her go, James," Mary finally interjected.

"Stay out of it, bitch."

Mary tried to scratch his face, but he pulled back in time and let go of Beverly's hair.

"Hey, Mary, turn around."

As Mary turned around to see what James wanted, he backhanded her face with his right hand.

"Didn't I tell you to stay out of it? Come on, Beverly, let's go."

Beverly glanced over at Mary who was rubbing her face. She turned around to James.

"James, why did you do that?"

"Because I can't stand it when you act like this and Mary's just encouraging it. Come on, Bev, let's go, OK? I've missed you."

"Are you OK, Mary?" Beverly asked.

"Yeah, go on, Beverly, get your jerk of a boyfriend out of here."

And Beverly mumbled something and let James open the passenger door as he led her to his car.

They were silent most of the way home. But by the time they had reached Victoria, as usual, Beverly had softened toward him and sat close to him.

"I can't stand the thought of you with anyone else, James."

"Don't worry, baby. You're my girl. Come on, I've missed

you."

They pulled into the shadows one block from Beverly's house and climbed into the back seat where James tenderly undressed Beverly and kissed her gently and told her for the first time that he loved her. They held each other tightly and rocked back and forth until both of them were spent. They lay in the back seat for a long time passionately making plans for the rest of the summer. They forgot about Mary with the swollen lip and Sally with the tears streaming down her face. There was no one in the universe but them for now.

CHAPTER TWENTY–ONE

"Mrs. Smith, it looks like you are about six weeks pregnant. I hope this is good news?" The doctor looked concerned as he gazed at the young girl with a simple gold band around her wedding finger.

"Oh, yes! Mr. Smith will be so pleased. Thank you, doctor." She played with the ring around her finger nervously.

The doctor left her alone to dress, and Karen smiled to herself wondering how and when she would break the news to Bill. It needed to be soon because she was supposed to leave for college in three weeks. That wouldn't be happening now although she knew that it would take a few months before he could be divorced and then marry her, but she could wait, even if the baby could not.

She looked forward to seeing the look on Bill's face when she told him. He had become increasingly dependent on her this summer. Even though he and his wife stayed out at the lake house, he managed to sneak away two or three times a week to meet Karen. They had been going to his house in town on occasion, but she could tell that it made him uncomfortable even though they never made love in the master bedroom. They never seemed to make it that far.

She smiled as she thought of their session the day before. She always walked to his house cutting through back yards. He lived at the end of the street and his back yard had a high fence around it. The gate faced an empty lot and whenever they met at the house, Bill left the gate unlocked, and Karen would slip inside unnoticed.

Yesterday, he stood at the sliding glass doors at the back of the house waiting for her with a beer in his hand. As soon as she had entered the house, he had grabbed her and pushed her up against the wall of the kitchen. He had ripped the top button off her knit top in his hurry to touch her breasts. When he had finally gotten to her bare skin, he pored beer over her naked nipples which were swollen and browner and larger with the onset of her pregnancy. He began sucking loudly from one side to the other while she reached down and found him swollen and stretching the fabric of his shorts. Soon she released him from his prison and caressed him until he couldn't stand it any longer. He didn't bother to remove either her skirt or panties but pulled both aside impatiently until the rip of the cotton underwear could be heard. He had entered her and finished before either had said a word.

Later when he was able, they went into the extra bedroom and took their time with their clothes off. Karen did whatever he wanted, and he wanted everything from her. They spent hours experimenting and examining every line and curve and crevice. Karen could see in his eyes the insatiable hunger that he had for her. She was thankful she didn't have to work that day.

Now Karen planned and plotted how and where she would tell him. She didn't want it to be at his wife's house or in the back seat of his Mustang. She wanted neutral ground befitting her status as the mother of his unborn child. His first child no less.

May and Hollis continued to meet throughout the summer. Although the spring had seen many deaths in Victoria, summer brought with it a languid sense of peacefulness and with the lassitude, few deaths occurred in the tiny hamlet. Hollis found himself with much time on his hands and spent most daylight hours down at the furniture store working on the books in the back office. During July, George and Susan took an extended trip around the United States with their two boys so Hollis was alone much of the time at the store. Martha also stayed away because she was supervising renovations around the house. Hollis had little patience for wallpaper patterns and carpet pile.

As a result, May had taken to coming down to the store in the late afternoons. In the summer, the store did little business, and Karen could handle most of the traffic in the showroom while Hollis handled the books and other things in the back office. Mostly July was a time to prepare for the major fall promotions which began appearing in August.

Sometimes when May arrived, Karen would be sweeping the

floors. May would come in through the back door and go directly
into the office. Karen very rarely saw her or knew that she was there.
Once she did arrive, Hollis would come out of the office and tell
Karen to lock up and go home since it didn't look like any more
customers would arrive. Then he would go into the office and lock
the door. May was usually perched on one of the chairs smiling
sweetly and provocatively swinging a nicely tanned leg. Hollis
would call Martha to find out how her day had gone, but mostly to
find out if she might be venturing out of the house to come downtown anytime soon. Usually he would catch Martha in the middle of
some mess with the painters, and she would quickly get him off the
line. Neither one of them thought to check on Johnny's whereabouts.

When they were sure they were alone and would not be
interrupted, they went over to the small couch. Often they would just
talk quietly for a few moments asking about the mundane and
intimate details of each other's lives. They would talk about things
they couldn't or wouldn't talk about in front of their families. It was
the talk of two lovers concerned about one another. Most of the time
their low murmurings would end with passionate love–making where
neither noticed the smallness of the couch or the cramped quarters of
the office and where neither forgot that they could be caught at any
moment.

Beverly had enjoyed her summer as well. James had returned from camp in the beginning of July, and they had spent
limited time with one another. As far as Beverly knew, he no longer
saw Sally. She really didn't want to know if he was seeing her either.

Beverly also worked with her church volunteering to go into
the migrant camps in the surrounding areas to teach the children to
read and write. They spent long Sunday afternoons playing games
with the children and teaching them crafts, too. For Beverly, the
experience opened her eyes to a whole other world where a house,
family, and food to eat were not guaranteed.

The parents of these children seldom ventured out of their
houses on Sundays, and on Wednesdays when they came to teach
lessons, the parents were out working in the sweltering sun to bring

in a tiny amount of money which mostly went toward beer and cigarettes. It broke Beverly's heart to know that she wouldn't see these beautiful children again after August when their families would move to another part of the country for the end of yet another growing season.

One Sunday, she asked Mrs. Kelly to come with her. Beverly and James' mother had been spending time together this past summer. Usually Beverly would drive out to see her in the afternoons while James worked out. They would shell peas, string beans, and can vegetables from Mrs. Kelly's garden. But most importantly, Beverly talked to her about herself and sometimes about James.

"Listen, Beverly, I know my son's got a temper so I hope he's treating you right," she said one afternoon as they peeled the skins off tomatoes.

"I try to keep him happy, but it's not always easy. I understand why he gets angry. Some people treat him horribly, you know. Some of them are in my family."

Mrs. Kelly sighed, "I was afraid of that. But, Beverly, that's not your fault. Don't let James hurt you. He's an awful lot like his daddy."

"Mr. Kelly? I've never heard James talk about him."

"That's because he don't know much about him and that's just fine. He left ten years ago after nearly killing me. See this scar?" She lifted up her chin to reveal a long white mark.

"He did that?" Beverly gasped.

"Yes, he did. And why? Because I told him he better start bringing home more money because I was pregnant again. He told me, 'don't you tell me I better do anything.'"

Beverly stared at her for a long time. "What happened to the baby?"

"I miscarried that night, but he wasn't around to help me. I sent James to get Mrs. Jones down the road. She's a midwife, and she helped me through it. James is better off not knowing about him."

"James says the same thing to me," Beverly said softly.

"Has he ever hit you?"

Beverly refused to answer.

When Mrs. Kelly came with her to the migrant camp, the other members of her group kept their distance. When Beverly tried to introduce her, they all nodded and then went to the field to start playing a game with the children.

"Where are the parents?" Mrs. Kelly asked Beverly ignoring the rudeness of these fine Christians.

"The mothers are usually in the cabins on Sundays. Sometimes the men are working or drinking."

"Let's go visit the women, and see if we can be of help in the kitchen. Maybe I can give them some hints."

No one had ever suggested that before, and Beverly thought it was a good idea. At first the women seemed reluctant to let them enter, but Mrs. Kelly was very persuasive and soon she was showing them how to feed more mouths on less rice by adding vegetables which they got from the owners.

"Beverly, it's not a good idea to go into their homes," one of the youth leaders told her as they walked to the cars that afternoon. "It's not seemly for someone like you to be inside with them. It's one thing for Mrs. Kelly to do it, but you shouldn't go with her."

Beverly ignored her and was glad that Mrs. Kelly had not heard.

James kept himself busy staying in shape. Since he also played football, training for that began intensely the first of August. However, both Beverly and James were content with the amount of time they had together. James did come over to her house occasionally when her parents were home. Martha Canon was always polite and gracious. Hollis, on the other hand, usually ignored his presence or when forced to speak, grunted his replies. Therefore, the day in late July when Hollis actually initiated a conversation with him, James felt uneasy.

"James, have any colleges been recruiting?" he asked in a friendly manner when James sat down in the living room one evening.

142

"Yes, Sir, I've heard from a few," James replied warily.

"Who looks good?"

"Well, Michigan would be my first choice, but they aren't offering much."

"What about MSU?"

"I've talked to a few coaches, but they haven't really pursued me like some of the smaller schools. MSU would be my next choice, though."

"What about out of state schools? Any interest there?"

"I've heard from the University of Indiana and Notre Dame, but not seriously. I'm not sure I want to be that far from home just yet, Sir." James wondered why the sudden interest.

"Well, James, you are one of the lucky ones, for sure. You can pretty much pick and choose where you want to go. I guess it depends on who offers the best deal, huh? You might not want to discount the out of state offers totally."

"That's true. I plan on going to a National Tournament in October where there'll probably be lots of recruiters. It's one of the reasons they hold these things for high school players."

"Where's that, James?"

"Uh, I think, in Indianapolis around the fifteenth of October. You know, if you and your family want to come, I'm sure I can get tickets," he suggested hesitantly.

"Well, maybe we'll think about that. My son Tom mentioned wanting to see you play. You know it was his record you broke in total career baskets in your junior year! Anyway, he couldn't make it for any games this year, but he's talked about the coach at Iowa showing interest in you, so maybe I'll mention the tournament to them."

"I know Tom Canon set a lot records at VHS, Sir. I promise I'll leave some intact when I leave." James allowed himself a small grin.

Hollis laughed a little at that attempt at a joke. Beverly walked in at that precise moment to find her boyfriend and father smiling at one another as if they liked each other! She was usually on

143

egg shells when James came to her house because she hated the awful way her father acted. Also when they left together after these painful encounters, James was always rude to her and sometimes would find excuses to fight. A few times he had hit her, but mostly he just verbally abused her. He'd say anything he could think of to wound her and belittle her. It usually worked. Once or twice he had taken it out on her sexually, but Beverly had learned to endure these sessions. She even understood why he acted the way he did, and felt that she somehow had to make it up to him for the way other people treated him.

This evening, however, when they left, James acted light–hearted though puzzled about her father's change in attitude.

"Maybe he just realized that he has been wrong all this time, James. My father's that way. He's so stubborn sometimes when things don't go his way. It just takes him awhile to come around. Besides I've noticed that he's happier these days, and I think he's drinking less because he doesn't go down to the funeral home basement as much as he used to," Beverly explained.

"Your father drinks!?" James loudly exclaimed.

"I thought everyone knew," Beverly said quietly. "It's usually worse when there have been lots of deaths. I don't think my father enjoys his job."

"Well, I didn't know. I thought your family was perfect. Isn't that what they expect from everyone else around them?"

"Looks can be deceiving. My father's been unhappy as long as I can remember. My mother doesn't allow alcohol in the house, though. And I guess as long as he isn't falling down drunk in the gutters of Victoria, everyone just looks the other way."

"Yeah, as long as his white skeletons are kept in the closet, huh?"

"Something like that, I guess. I know my parents are hypo-crites if that's what you mean. I've known it for awhile now. I'm just sorry that some of it has to involve you."

"Don't worry, Bev, I'll survive. And maybe there's hope. Your dad was pretty friendly tonight. He said they might even come to Indiana to see me play in October."

"You're kidding?" Beverly smiled. "Maybe things are looking up after all."

And then she grabbed James's face and turned it toward her and gave him the gentlest of kisses imaginable.

CHAPTER TWENTY–TWO

While George was away on his trip, Hollis came to depend on Karen more and more to handle things in the store. He knew she would be leaving for school soon, and he wondered who they could ever find to replace her. She had been the most responsible high school student that they had ever hired.

"Listen, Karen, can you stay and do a little extra work today? It would mean extra hours," Hollis asked Karen one early August afternoon.

"What do you want done, Mr. Canon?"

"Well, next week the new fall line will arrive, and I'd like the showroom spic and span when it gets here. I was wondering if after you swept today, you could go ahead and mop the floors and maybe apply some wax before you go home."

"Sure, I can use the extra money, what with college and all. Do you want me to call you when I finish so you can come down and lock up?"

"No, why don't you just take this extra key? I may have some other things for you to do before next week. Then after the furniture arrives, there will be some extra work, too. Now, when did you say you were leaving for Central?"

"I leave in two weeks. Thanks for the key, Mr. Canon. I'll be sure to give it back before I leave."

After Hollis had gone, Karen diligently mopped the floor. While she waited for it to dry, she went into the office and called Bill at his summer cottage. When he answered, she sighed in relief and told him she needed him to come into town because they needed to talk about something very important.

"I told you not to call me here," Bill hissed quietly into the receiver.

"It's important, or I wouldn't have called. Come to the side

146

door of the furniture store, the one that faces Center Street. It'll be unlocked. I'm all alone here. No one is coming back tonight because I have the key to lock up after I finish with the floors. Please?" she pleaded.

"OK, give me an hour." And with that, he slammed the phone down.

Karen went about her job humming to herself imagining how she would break the news. She knew he would be overjoyed since his wife had yet to provide him with a child. And she knew Bill loved her.

"All right, Karen, what is so god awful important that you made me lie to my wife?" Bill demanded when he arrived.

"Sit down, Bill. Come on into the showroom. No one can see us from the street if we sit back here. See, isn't this couch comfortable. Relax," Karen cooed as she pulled him down next to her on the leather couch.

He became aroused as her soft voice caressed him, and the leather gave off a masculine musty smell and enveloped his body in its arms. He reached for Karen and began kissing her and tugging at her blouse.

"Stop it, Bill! I've got something to tell you. That can wait."

"Not really, baby. See, I can't wait." He pulled her hand down on top of his pants, and she immediately saw what he meant. She leaned down and gave him some relief so she could continue. Otherwise, she knew he would never leave her alone long enough to listen.

"Now please, Bill, let's talk. We always do that. You know we will, but first I have to tell you something."

Bill looked at her between half closed eyes as he rubbed his hands over her swollen breasts. Suddenly he sat up straight and removed his hands when he saw the glow and twinkle in her eyes. Something was up all right, and suddenly it wasn't him.

"OK, shoot."

"I'm pregnant," she gushed.

Silence permeated the showroom.

"Bill, I just said I was pregnant. Say something."

"I don't know what to say. What happened to the birth control pills you got?"

She had already anticipated this question. "My mother found them early this summer and threw them out."

"Why didn't you tell me?"

"I didn't want to upset you, and I was afraid you wouldn't want to be with me again. I love you, Bill."

"Karen, how far along?"

"About six or seven weeks, I think. Aren't you happy?"

"I'm surprised. Give me a moment to think. Does anyone else know?"

"Of course not! I'd never tell anyone else before I told you!" she cried.

"Good, good. What doctor did you see?"

"I went to a doctor in East Lansing last week. I told them my name was Mrs. Smith. I've been waiting to find the perfect time to tell you and when Mr. Canon asked. . ."

"OK, OK, now let's think. No one knows anything about this, right?" Bill interrupted.

"No, I told you. . . Why?"

"That's good. Well, something like this we can't just let get out. We've got to plan."

"Oh, Bill, that's what I was thinking. I know everything will take some time to sort out."

"Right, right. Now, Karen, you leave for school in two weeks?" Karen nodded. "OK, you just go on up to Mt. Pleasant and start the semester while I stay here and work things out."

"But how can I go to college when I'm pregnant?" Karen was beginning to think that maybe things weren't going to go as she had imagined.

"You probably won't show for some time. And when you start putting on weight, you can just start wearing larger clothes. It's not unusual to put on ten pounds or so when you first start eating dorm food. That should get us through until the holidays. And by then, I'll have found a place for you to go to have the baby which should come in March or so, right?"

"Right, but what about us?"

"Us? Oh, right. Well, listen things can't happen overnight now, Karen. Just be patient. I can't really do anything until this year's basketball season is over. You must understand that. This year will be James' last, and he has a great chance for a full basketball scholarship to a Big Ten school. Also we may win another state championship. No school has ever done that! Then after that I can write my own ticket. I might be able to get a coaching job at a larger school or even in a college. We can't do anything to upset that, now can we? Too many lives would be ruined."

Karen nodded numbly. So she would go away until basketball season ended and then they would be married, she thought. She could handle that. Once the team won state championship again, they could move anywhere they wanted.

"Do you understand, baby? I want to be with you so much, but we have to wait," Bill pleaded.

"I understand, just tell me what I should do and where I should go. I can wait until spring, and then we'll have a son or daughter to enjoy, too." She kissed him lightly on the forehead and began to rub the front of his pants where there was no longer a bulge. He pushed her hand away.

"Baby, I've got a lot to think about. I'd better go now or I'll blow my cover." And for the first time in almost a year, he didn't feel the need to possess Karen completely before he left her.

Karen walked him to the back door and then watched him walk to his car. He hadn't said he wouldn't marry her.

Bill Hoover carefully backed out of the parking space behind Canon Furniture Store. He drove mechanically while sweating profusely. He needed time to think. How could this have happened in the best year of his career? He'd be ruined if anyone found out that he had gotten a high school girl pregnant. Managing Karen would be his most difficult task in the months ahead. He thought about abortion but quickly put the thought out of his mind. Too dangerous and costly and illegal. But if he found a home for her to wait out the final months of her pregnancy, the baby could easily be put up for adoption. He had months to bring up the subject to Karen and convince her that this baby needed to be brought up in a family with both a mother and father.

He knew that Karen thought he was going to marry her in the spring. He needed her to continue to think that so she would keep quiet. All in all, he thought he had handled the situation admirably considering how shocked he had been when she told him.

After stopping at the store for something for his wife, he drove through Victoria and saw James going into the Canon house. He honked his horn and waved. He sure wished James would start dating someone of his own kind. He hid it very well, but he thought that what James and Beverly were doing was an act against God.

Then he wondered who he might have as an office aide during the coming school year. No one came immediately to mind, and for the first time since he started teaching, he considered not having an aide or at least not one who attracted him. He had made a mistake with Karen, one he hoped wasn't fatal. He'd have to be more careful and since he would have to deal with both Karen and Alice more carefully this year, maybe a year off wouldn't be a bad idea.

He shook his head and drove on through the early evening. The warm summer air cleared his head as he headed back to his cozy cottage by the lake shared by his wife of six years who waited patiently for him to return with her ice cream which she had been craving endlessly for the last month.

CHAPTER TWENTY–THREE

As autumn approached, few changes took place in Victoria except upon the trees whose leaves began to change into glorious paintings against a blue sky background. Reds, oranges, and yellows burst forth upon the community in splendor that fall of 1971. Not until the end of October would everyone be brought back abruptly to reality as the leaves fell to the ground creating the stark naked look of death for all to see. Endlessly, people would rake those leaves, and by October all the town would be filled with the smell of burning leaves and burnt marshmallows. They all thought it extremely crucial to rake those leaves before the tons of snow fell directly upon the dormant grass.

Karen left town for Mt. Pleasant and Central Michigan University near the end of August. She would be nearly three hours from home. Her parents would probably not come to visit again, and already she had resigned herself to not seeing Bill or Victoria until the Thanksgiving holidays when she would take a Greyhound home. After she had told Bill her news, she had only seen him once before she left. They didn't touch, but he seemed concerned about her health and told her to take care of herself and his baby. She knew she had overwhelmed him with her news, but she also knew that he cared about her.

George and Hollis both missed Karen. By the end of September, they still hadn't found a replacement for her so Susan had been helping whenever needed. Sometimes even Martha would come down to help out when the funeral home was active. Two generations of Canons found themselves juggling both businesses. Things became so hectic that finally they decided Beverly could help out after school on some afternoons particularly when a body lay in state up at the funeral home. She didn't mind. James was working hard on the football field, and they only spent sporadic moments together.

May knew Hollis couldn't fit her into his busy schedule so she put little pressure on him. They did manage to work in a few meetings in the evenings that autumn. However, it became increasingly dangerous because the whole Canon family now had business to do at the store.

Beverly noticed one late afternoon in September that her Aunt May had come into the office. Beverly had just finished sweeping and was putting away the broom in the back utility closet. Her position kept her hidden from view of the back door, so May didn't see her standing there behind the closet door when she quietly knocked on the office door and then went quickly inside. Beverly heard the click of the lock behind May. Puzzled she went to the door and listened. She knew her father hadn't left yet; they had talked about walking home together. As she leaned closer to the door she could hear soft muffled voices and then quiet.

Concerned she knocked on the door. Her father quickly unlocked and opened the door a crack.

"Yes, what is it, Beverly?"

"I wondered if everything was OK. I saw Aunt May come in the office, and she seemed upset. Besides, I'm done sweeping, and I thought we were walking home together."

Aunt May appeared as Hollis opened the door further. "I was just going. Your father was helping me out with a little domestic problem, Beverly. Sorry we kept you waiting. Bye, Hollis, Beverly." And May swept out of the office and out the back door.

Beverly's father shuffled his feet and refused to make eye contact with his daughter. Beverly looked closely at him and wondered what had just happened.

"Is everything all right with Aunt May and Uncle Johnny?"

"Sure, sure, Bev. Just the same old stuff. Now let's go home."

Beverly wasn't the only person confused about May. Johnny Randall still felt uneasy around his wife, but his memory seemed dimmer than ever. He didn't have the same lust for life that had always characterized him. He didn't even have the will to keep May

152

in line anymore, but maybe that was because May acted differently these past few months. She never talked back, and if he did complain about something, she quietly tried to change whatever he didn't like. And she always seemed to be smiling.

He decided that the next time she left after dinner, he would follow her. He vowed to stay sober enough in the evenings so he could discover where she went.

Hollis and May decided to meet the very next night after Beverly had gone home. He told Martha he had to have the quarterly reports done so not to keep supper. He had really missed May. It had been nearly two weeks since their last encounter.

May told Johnny that she needed a walk after supper. She knew he didn't care when she would be home since he'd most likely be passed out by then anyway. However, May hadn't noticed that Johnny had cut back on his drinking before and after supper.

As she slipped out of the house, Johnny watched from the bedroom window. When she reached the corner, she turned right towards downtown. Johnny left the house and began following her. When she reached the corner before Canon Furniture Store, she took another right and then crossed the street heading into the alley behind that block's stores. Curiosity eating at him, Johnny reached the alley just as May slipped in the back door of the furniture store. He went around to the front and saw no lights on inside. He went to the back again and noticed no cars parked back there either. He shrugged his shoulders and decided that it must be some family matter, and he went back home.

When he reached his house, he poured himself a long drink and sucked it down reverently. On impulse he called the Canon's house. He was surprised when Martha answered.

"Uh, hey, Martha, this is Johnny. You seen May?"

"No, not tonight, Johnny. Why? Is something wrong?"

"Oh, it's nothing. I just thought she was coming over to see you and Hollis. Maybe she said Connie's house instead."

"No, Johnny. I'm here alone. Hollis is down at the store working on the quarterly reports. If I hear from May, I'll tell her you're looking for her."

"Sure, thanks, Martha." Johnny thoughtfully hung up the phone. Martha is sitting at home, and Hollis is down at the furniture store with May which Martha doesn't know, he thought. Then slowly the fog began to lift as he pictured May and Hollis alone together in the office. That picture in his mind suddenly changed into another image of Hollis and May, only this time they weren't at the store but on the embalming table at the funeral home, and they weren't working on any books. He could see May's face and bare arms as they reached up around the back of Hollis who lay naked upon his wife.

He threw his empty glass at the wall in front of him and swore loudly. Now he knew why Hollis and May always seemed to be keeping some secret from the rest of them as they talked quietly at family gatherings and why May had been rather complacent around the house for months now. He took the bottle with him into the living room and guzzled the vodka as fast as he could to wipe out the image of his naked wife and brother–in–law as they groped for one another in the night.

CHAPTER TWENTY–FOUR

As September turned into October, Beverly became increasingly bothered about her father and May. A few memories kept edging their way to the front of her consciousness as she struggled to make sense of it all.

Her mother never mentioned any problems with May and Johnny after the encounter at the store a few weeks earlier. Usually May came to her sister to confide the ebb and flow of her tidal wave marriage. It didn't make sense that Beverly's father would be her confessor. However, Beverly knew better than to ask her mother about this one.

Beverly tried to push it to the back of her mind while enjoying the fall season and her junior year of high school. She had tried out for the junior play and won a secondary role as a young married woman. She was enjoying herself immensely and threw herself into the role. She didn't want to think about anything unpleasant. James and she had fallen into an easy relationship and once again she felt that he was her best friend.

One night she decided to tell James about her suspicions about her father and Aunt May. She hesitated because she hated giving him more fuel for his anger against her family. But maybe he would convince her that she was imagining things. Or maybe he would have a logical explanation for what she had seen.

She told James about the incident in the office. He didn't say anything for a long time.

"Is this it? You suspect something fishy because of this one time?" he finally asked.

"Well, there are other things that I started remembering. Both of their behaviors were strange that day. And besides my mom hasn't said anything about any problems with Aunt May and Uncle Johnny. She usually goes on and on about poor May whenever something happens. She seems to really enjoy Aunt May's problems. And Aunt May almost always confides in my mom first."

"And what else?" James wasn't satisfied.

"I keep remembering one night a few months ago. I came home from church and when I drove by the funeral home, Aunt May's car was parked outside the basement door. I assumed Mom and she were down there doing something. Yet when I came home, Mom was watching TV. I put it out of my mind, but now it keeps coming back."

"Was your father home, too?"

"No, I can't remember where he was," Beverly said sadly.

"Anything else?" James inquired again.

"Just moments that I remember now seeing Dad and Aunt May talking quietly together at family gatherings. I remember thinking on Memorial Day that they seemed especially close. At the time, I thought it was so nice that they had put the past behind them."

"What do you mean?"

"I never finished telling you, did I? Remember once I told you that Dad and Aunt May almost got married? Well, I wasn't really exaggerating. I guess they were kind of engaged. It's a big family joke about how Aunt May liked Uncle Johnny's car better so she broke up with my dad. And then my mom began chasing after my dad until he noticed her."

James let out a long breath of air between pursed lips. He just shook his head for awhile before saying anything. "Your family beats all. They act so almighty perfect and then all this secret stuff keeps spilling out of your mouth. The scary thing is you don't even realize what it all means."

Beverly started to protest, but then thought better of disagreeing. She needed James right now. Maybe his objective perspective could help.

"Beverly, don't you see? Your dad and Aunt May have probably been having an affair all these years. All the while both of them acting better than poor black folk like me and making you feel like a piece of crap for dating me." He continued to shake his head

156

sadly.

"No, James! I don't believe it. I–I think maybe my dad and Aunt May. . ." she trailed off when it became clear that she couldn't think of any way to respond.

"What, you think Daddy and Aunt May were just comforting one another for making a mistake so many years ago. I'd like that kind of comforting myself."

"No, I don't believe it. My dad would never . . . Aunt May maybe . . . I don't know." Beverly ran out of steam as she sat next to James in the car trying to make sense out of all of it.

"Listen, baby, I know you don't want to believe the worst about your family, but it's time you began facing some truths. Your family isn't perfect."

"James, I know that. I told you about my dad and his drinking. My mom is so cold to him sometimes, and then my dad is so stubborn. But aren't everyone's parents like that?"

"But everyone's parents aren't as judgmental as yours. My mom isn't. Yet I know she would never have sex with her brother–in–law."

"Stop, James. I can't think about that now. Take me home. I just want to think over everything."

James leaned over and kissed her gently. He started the car and backed it carefully out of the parking space on the side of the dirt road on the outskirts of Victoria. He wouldn't push Beverly anymore tonight, but he knew as well as he knew his name that Hollis Canon and May Randall were more than just relatives by marriage.

When James dropped her off, Beverly found her mother sitting alone in the living room watching "Laugh–In" usually one of Beverly's favorite shows.

"Where's Dad?" she inquired when she came into the room.

"Oh, he had some catching up to do down at the store. With the funeral last week, he got behind in the paperwork. I wish he would just hire someone to do that, but no, he wants to do it all himself." She sighed and returned to watching TV.

157

Patricia C. Behnke

"Listen, Mom, I'm still wound up, and it's such a pretty night, I think I'll walk down to the store and see if I can't get Dad to come home with me."

Martha Canon barely heard her daughter and just waved her out the door. Beverly stopped by the key hooks at the back door and took the set marked, "Store".

Beverly circled the store several times before letting herself in the back door. There were no cars parked out back, but that didn't mean anything. Her father had walked, and Aunt May lived within walking distance.

As she came into the darkened hallway, the light from underneath the closed office door served as a beacon for Beverly as she fumbled for the key to the office. She hesitated for long moments wondering if she should knock. First, she decided to quietly test the door knob. If her father was really in there just working, he wouldn't lock the door. After a quick test, she discovered that indeed the door was locked. She couldn't hear much, just some muffled sounds indistinguishable as words.

Without any further doubt, she put the key in the lock and turned it. In a fog, she opened the door and found what James had known she would find. Her father and her aunt on the couch partially undressed kissing one another oblivious to the fact that the door had opened. Her aunt's breasts were exposed and her father was leaning down kissing one of them while May worked on pulling off Hollis' shirt. Beverly remained paralyzed while the truth sunk into her consciousness. Still, the couple mesmerized by only themselves, were unaware that they had an audience.

Quickly Beverly pulled the door closed not bothering to be quiet when she shut it. Blindly she ran back out the door and into the alley sobbing and choking and stumbling.

Hollis Canon pulled himself away from May at the sound of the office door slamming. He quickly got up from the couch and fumbled for his shoes. May had managed to remove his shirt although he still had on his undershirt. Without bothering to put on the shirt, he opened the back door of the store finding his only daughter

158

Beverly leaning up against the building next door screaming and crying at the same time.

"Beverly, I. . . " he slowly approached her.

"Get away from me," she screamed. "You didn't even bother to get dressed," she managed when she finally turned to look at her father exposed in his undershirt and untied shoes.

"Beverly, please, let's be reasonable," Hollis pleaded.

"Reasonable, REASONABLE! You expect me to be reasonable, and you're in there with your wife's sister and. . ." She exploded into tears again as she remembered the awful image of two people she had loved and respected all her life.

"What are you going to do with this information, Beverly?" May had come up silently to the tiny group.

"Do with this information? My how polite we all are! You two are pathetic." With that Beverly turned and began walking down the street toward home leaving the two lovers speechless and alone in the darkened alley.

CHAPTER TWENTY–FIVE

Beverly took a circuitous route home to compose herself. She didn't know what to do with her new–found information, but she knew she couldn't tell her mother. She quietly let herself in the back door.

"Is that you, Hollis?" Martha yelled from the living room.

"No, Mom, it's me. Dad's still at work. I couldn't get him to come home with me," Beverly lied.

"OK, are you feeling all right, Beverly?" her mother inquired as Beverly made her way through the living room to her bedroom.

"I'm just awfully tired. This play is really taking a toll on me. I can't seem to get my lines straight in Act Two. 'Night, Mom."

"'Night, dear," her innocent mother called from her chair.

Beverly slept little that night, but May and Hollis slept even less. Hollis actually ended up in the basement of the funeral home feeling lower than he had ever felt. Since he and May had begun seeing one another, he had found less and less reason to visit the embalming room. However, tonight he saw no other alternative as he pondered what his daughter might do.

May sat up watching the late show most of the night. Johnny had been surly and uncommunicative, more so than usual in the last few weeks, and she had walked on egg shells around him. Tonight he had drunk himself into a stupor by the time she had managed to make it home, thank goodness. She couldn't face a confrontation with him tonight. She felt light–headed every time she thought about Beverly telling Martha about what she had discovered. She waited for the phone to ring most of the night.

Beverly managed to stay away from her father for the next week. The night after her discovery, the former mayor of Victoria died, and so Hollis was caught up in providing a prominent citizen all the rites of death accorded him by his previous position.

160

The National High School Basketball Tournament was coming up in a week, and Beverly planned on traveling to Indianapolis with the Browns to see James play. Her parents had toyed with the idea of going, but Beverly had discouraged it from the beginning. She did find out that her brother Tom would be there along with the head basketball coach from Iowa State. James seemed pleased that the head coach was coming. Most colleges sent recruiters or assistants.

Martha Canon was beginning to have doubts about the advisability of Beverly going so far away from home with James and the Brown family who she didn't quite trust since she hadn't known them since birth.

One morning while Hollis, Martha, and Beverly grabbed quick breakfasts, Martha brought up the subject.

"You know, Beverly, I'm not so sure you should go on this trip next week if we aren't going, too," Martha began.

"What do you mean? They've already made reservations for me. I'm staying in a room with the kids adjoining the Browns. Tom's staying in the same motel."

"Well, I'm just not sure about the situation. Don't you agree, Hollis?" Martha glanced at her husband for support.

Beverly looked directly at her father for the first time in a week, giving him a cool, disdainful look. He couldn't hold her gaze.

"Yes, Father, what do you think? Do you think that this is a moral question? Do you think that going on this trip will cause a scandal?" Beverly asked sweetly.

Hollis turned away from his daughter's saccharine demeanor.

"I think Beverly will be fine, Martha. We already said she could go," he said firmly.

"But. . ." Martha sputtered at her husband's lack of backbone response. What had happened to him? When it came to Beverly and James, he always sided with her.

"That's final, Martha, let it go."

Beverly smiled smugly as she kissed the top of her mother's

161

head before leaving for school. Her eyes met those of her father's. He understood exactly what she meant. As long as he didn't cross Beverly, his secret would be safe.

James and Beverly left for Indianapolis, Indiana driving one of the Browns' cars. The Browns followed closely in their station wagon with the kids in the back seat. Coach Hoover would come the following morning before the first tournament game at 11:00 a.m.

As they sped south on I–69, Beverly finally told James what she had discovered about her father and Aunt May. He didn't seem surprised or sympathetic.

"I told you, Bev, your family is full of it. The sooner you're away from them the better. It's a wonder you aren't more messed up than you already are."

Beverly decided to ignore that remark and just enjoy being alone with James. She didn't want anything to spoil their weekend together. Except for not sharing a room, this weekend would be almost like they were married, and while they drove along side by side, she could pretend they were newlyweds leaving for their honeymoon.

When they arrived at the motel, they found Tom in the lobby checking in along with Kasey Backus, the coach from Iowa.

"Tom! Hi, this is James," Beverly said as she reached up to give her big brother a hug.

"Hi, Beverly, James. This is Kasey Backus. What are you two doing for dinner?" Tom asked.

"I was hoping we could eat with you wherever you want," Beverly said.

"That's what I was hoping, too. James, since you've got the big day tomorrow, what's your preference?" Tom gave his full attention to the very tall basketball star.

"Well, a steak sounds good to me. There's a Western Steer across the street. I'm a little tired of driving."

"Good, let's check in and meet back here in say an hour?" Kasey asked good–naturedly.

The dinner went well. Tom and James hit it off trading

162

stories and bantering back and forth about records and which ones James might break again this year. Coach Backus interjected information every so often about Iowa, and James listened politely. But so far nothing had been offered.

The next morning, Bill Hoover arrived and spent a few moments with James before the game began.

"Just remember, James, you are the best. Don't be intimidated because these guys are as tall as you. You've got the best moves in the game as long as you keep your mind on the ball," Coach counseled as James suited up.

"Thanks, Coach. It does feel a little weird to no longer be the tallest guy around, but I'll be fine. I'm feeling real loose and cool," James said as he put on his warm–up jacket.

James played one of his best games yet. Kasey Backus was impressed. Even with the other talent on the court, James managed to score twenty points and rebound twenty–four times. He truly looked as if he was born to play the sport with his natural ease and agility as he jumped and ran down the court.

After the game, both Hoover and Backus caught up with James as he headed to the locker room. They asked him to come into the conference room next door after he finished dressing to have a little talk.

James showered and hurried with his business. He knew he had played his best game and held his own against some of the best basketball players in the nation. He felt confident as he headed toward the conference room. He could hear the two coaches and Tom laughing loudly at something as he came near the door.

"Well, I think it would be a great relief to everyone in Victoria if you could convince James to come to Iowa," he heard Bill Hoover remark.

"Oh, yeah? Why?" Kasey asked.

"Oh, James is pretty serious with Tom's sister and that's got everyone in an uproar in town. I think the Canons especially would be happier if he left the area after next year and left Beverly alone," Bill offered.

"That's pretty much the whole picture, Kasey. I didn't tell you before because I thought you should see James play, but Mom and Dad are pushing for him to go out of state. They hope Beverly will forget all about the relationship if he's 500 miles away," Tom continued.

"Well, I don't care about any of that. I've got a basketball program to run, and James Kelly is the best new talent I've seen in years. I plan on making him an offer he can't refuse and it is not because of your parents, Tom," Kasey said emphatically.

But James had already left by the time Kasey's final words on the subject. He felt himself teetering out of control as he searched for the nearest exit.

He had one more game to play that night, and then they planned on driving all night back to Victoria arriving early Sunday morning. James stayed away from the arena and the motel until game time. No one knew where he had gone or if he would even show up for the game.

Beverly, worried sick, began to grow weary of all the questions about his whereabouts. It was as if everyone thought she had hidden him or kidnapped him. She had no idea what had happened to him. He was fine when he had left that morning.

The Browns, Beverly, Tom, Kasey, and Bill heaved one collective sigh of relief when they saw James run onto the court for the pregame drill. Only Beverly noticed that he didn't seek her out in the stands for his traditional slight wave and smile.

After the game, when Beverly and the rest tried to congratulate James on his win and great playing, he shunned them all and headed for the Browns' car. Beverly said good–bye to her brother and followed reluctantly. She found herself scared to be alone with James, but knew she had no choice.

"James, honey, what's wrong?" she implored as soon as the car doors shut behind them.

"Shut up," he muttered.

Once he hit the highway, he pulled a bottle of Jack Daniels out of his bag directly behind the driver's seat. He took a long swig.

164

"James, please talk to me, you're scaring me." Beverly tried one more time to get him to open up. "I thought everything was going fine. You played great, and I heard Coach Backus was ready to make you an offer."

"I bet he was, I just bet he was. Did your brother or your father set up the deal, Beverly? Or was your father too busy hitting on your aunt? Or maybe it was your mother who set it up while sister dear gave it to her husband? Your family takes the crown." With that James pulled off the highway and down a deserted road.

"James, please, let's just keep driving. I'll drive if you're too tired. You've had a big day."

"Yeah, I've had a big day, Beverly, finding out that your father and mother and brother set Kasey Backus up to making me an offer to buy me out of Victoria and your life." James reached over and back–handed Beverly across the left cheekbone.

"James, what are you talking about? Don't hit me anymore, please, James, I love you," Beverly began sobbing now in earnest.

"Love me, you love me? I'll show you love, baby, the kind of love your family taught me."

And James spent his anger on Beverly somewhere in Indiana before getting back on the highway, but not before Beverly stopped crying and bleeding.

CHAPTER TWENTY–SIX

Beverly dosed off and on against the window of the passenger door as James drove through most of the night. Much of his anger had dissipated as dawn began creeping up on the horizon. When it was light enough to see, he saw Beverly, bruised and battered with a streaked face staring straight ahead on the highway. He pulled over at the next rest area.

"I'm sorry, Beverly, I just get so mad at you and your family. Come on, let's go in and find something to drink in the machines," James coaxed as he gently pulled the hair back from her face.

Beverly numbly shook her head. "Back seat," she managed to mumble.

James helped her into the back seat where she lay down. He covered her with his coat and began the rest of the drive back to Victoria.

It was around six o'clock when she let herself into the quiet house. Her parents would still be sleeping. She cleaned herself up a bit and then sat in the living room waiting for them to wake up.

"Beverly, you're home. . .What happened to your face?" Her mother asked horrified at what she saw sitting on the couch.

"What happened to my face is your fault. How could you set Coach Backus up to recruit James so he would leave town?"

"Who told you that?" Hollis quietly asked.

"James overheard a conversation yesterday with Hoover, Backus, and Tom, that's who told us," Beverly announced.

"But, Beverly, you still haven't told us what happened to your face!" Martha began to raise her voice.

"I had an accident, all right?! Leave me alone! You've done enough damage already." Beverly stormed into her bedroom.

Her father followed, slowly opening the hastily shut door. "Beverly, did James do this to you?" he asked.

"It's really none of your business," came the quick reply.

"It is our business. I've told you from the very beginning James is rotten to the core. What kind of animal would do this to another human being? I want you to stop seeing him now!" Hollis finally raised his voice.

"Oh, yeah? Well, listen, dear daddy, you lost your right to discipline me when I caught you quite literally with your pants down with my mother's sister! So get out of this room and leave me alone and find someone else to hand down pronouncements to," she screamed as Hollis slowly backed out of the room, incredulous at what his love for May had wrought.

Fortunately for Beverly, she had the play to occupy her time for the next month. No one said anything to her about her face. Even Laura knew better than to pry when she saw the determined set to Beverly's jaw. By the end of the week, all that remained on her face were slight yellowish bruises. Because the play had a holiday theme, the final performance would be held on the Wednesday before Thanksgiving.

Beverly, wounded on both the inside and out, kept blaming herself for James' anger. Those thoughts surfaced several times during each day, and she soon forgave James. He felt ashamed of his actions, and it pained him to look at Beverly even after the bruises healed. She walked with her shoulders drooping and her head hanging most of the time. And for the first few weeks after the attack, she ducked every time he tried to come near her.

One night several weeks later, James brought Beverly home from play practice. As they sat parked outside of her house, James reached for her to kiss her good night. Beverly pulled her face away from him as his arms swung out.

"Beverly, what's wrong? Why did you duck?"

"I don't know just a reaction. I'm sorry." She leaned toward him.

"I'm sorry, Beverly. Everytime I try to touch you, you back away. Are you that scared of me?"

"No, of course not. I love you, James." And she gave him a

long kiss before opening the car door and going inside.

Her mother waited for her along with her father.

"Beverly, who brought you home?"

"James. Why?"

"You're seeing him again? I thought we told you to stay away from him."

"Well, you didn't. Yes, I'm seeing him. I never stopped."

"Hollis, do something. We can't let her keep going out with him. Please tell her," Martha pleaded to her husband's open newspaper.

"She can make her own decisions," he said quietly without removing the paper.

The next day Martha called May.

"Where have you been, May? How come we don't see you anymore?" Martha asked when her sister finally answered the phone.

"Oh, I've been busy. Johnny's been on a rampage lately and you know, I can't get out much when that happens," May lied. "How are you, Martha?"

"Well, I'm worried about both Beverly and Hollis. Beverly is so hostile and continues to see that boy even after he's treated her so badly. And then Hollis! I don't know what to do about him," Martha exclaimed.

"What do you mean?"

"He won't stand up to Beverly. He just tells me that she can make her own decisions. He's home most of the time now in the evening but he doesn't talk to either one of us at all."

"Listen, Martha, I'm sorry you're having troubles, but Johnny just walked in the door, and I've really got to go," May told her quickly.

Martha hung up the phone even more puzzled and troubled than before. May seemed to be suffering from the same illness as the rest of her family.

By the time the play opened, Beverly had regained some of her confidence and told herself that now that she had stood up to her father, James would no longer be angry with her, and they would

168

have a good life.

James had a hard time forgetting and forgiving the Canons and kept away from their house and avoided Coach Hoover whenever possible. He wondered how he would manage to get through the season with Bill Hoover giving him advice and calling the shots. He'd thought often of switching schools as a solution, but he didn't want to leave Beverly.

Johnny Randall had been watching May, but noticed that during the past month she had not gone out at all during the evenings. He also noticed that she had very little to do with her extended family during this time.

As usual Grandma Stuart would be planning a huge family dinner for Thanksgiving Day with enough football on TV to create even larger appetites than usual. Beverly didn't even bother inviting James, but he had suggested that they both drive out to his mother's house for dinner, and Beverly gladly took him up on the suggestion. She couldn't imagine spending the day with her father, mother, and Aunt May all in the same room. She hadn't spent much time with Mrs. Kelly since school started and longed to sit and talk to her. Beverly knew Mrs. Kelly would coddle and spoil her and James all day long which was just fine with Beverly. Also, she and James' relationship always improved after a day at Ravens Wood Lake.

Karen came home for the holiday break on the Saturday before Thanksgiving. On Monday, she visited Victoria High and saw Bill for the first time since August. When she came into the office, she noticed Sheila Stone working at a small table near Bill's desk. Sheila could have been Karen's sister so closely did they resemble one another in coloring and build.

"Karen, it's good to see you!" Bill said as she came into his office that afternoon. "Listen, Sheila, could you run down to the front office and copy those tests? Thanks."

Sheila looked at Karen for a long time before picking up the papers and heading out the door. Karen didn't even notice her, she was so happy to see Bill.

"You look good, Karen. Are you still. . .?" he asked after

they were alone.

Karen let the question hang in the air for a few moments. "Of course, I'm still pregnant! Can't you tell? I've put on so much weight, but so far I've been able to hide it with these big CMU sweatshirts. The only good thing is the size of my boobs." She turned sideways for his inspection.

"Yeah, I noticed. Listen, we probably need to talk while you're home. I never feel right discussing things on the phone. I can probably get away Thanksgiving night. We're going to have a houseful of guests, so I can manage to sneak out without anyone noticing, OK?"

"I can manage that, I think. Listen, we can meet at the furniture store again if you want. I never gave the Canons my key back, and they'll all be too busy with their families to come by the store," Karen offered.

"OK, let's say around eight?"

"Fine. Bill, I miss you."

"Me, too, baby, me, too," Bill replied as he showed her out the door.

Karen decided to go to the play on Wednesday night. Several of her friends had parts, and she had heard that Beverly was really good. She didn't know that Bill would be there, too, with his wife.

She saw him standing in the hall during intermission talking to a short woman with her back to Karen. She started to wave and walk toward them when the woman turned around and looked directly at Karen.

"Hi, Karen, good to see you," said Alice Hoover. Bill had turned a quiet shade of red.

"Hi, Mrs. Hoover, nice to see you," Karen managed before turning abruptly away from the very pregnant form of Bill Hoover's wife.

CHAPTER TWENTY–SEVEN

Johnny watched May and Hollis all day at the family gathering on Thanksgiving Day. They didn't even seem to notice one another, and he hadn't seen them talking alone all day. He began to relax some and even enjoy the game being broadcast in the living room.

He didn't see May follow Hollis out to the kitchen later in the day after all the dishes had been cleaned away. They were only there alone for a minute, long enough for May to tell Hollis she had to see him very soon.

"How about tonight at the store? Martha will be tired and Beverly's out with James until whenever she feels like coming home," Hollis said sadly.

"I'm sorry about that, Hollis. But, yes tonight around 7:30? It's really important." And May went back into the living room unobserved by her husband.

Karen spent the whole miserable day in her room refusing to eat any of the dinner prepared by her very tired mother. She had no appetite and couldn't stop crying every time she thought about seeing Alice Hoover standing there in all of her pregnant glory. She didn't know what she would say to Bill tonight, if he even showed up.

Bill spent his day entertaining many family members of all ages. But at the back of his mind, he kept remembering Karen's face last night when she saw Alice's body. He hadn't thought about Karen going to anything at the high school while she was home, but he knew he should have kept his wife away. He didn't look forward to the evening ahead, but he knew he needed to keep calm because he had prodigious amounts of persuading to do in a few hours.

May pulled Johnny away from the TV at her mother's around 6 p.m. Once at home he noticed that she went immediately into the bathroom and began drawing a bath. When she emerged from the bathroom 45 minutes later she was fully dressed and made up. He pretended to drink in front of the TV.

"Johnny, I really need to walk off all of that food I ate today," she announced at 7:20.

"See ya later," Johnny slurred from the couch.

As soon as the door shut, Johnny headed to the garage. He pulled his car onto a side street and headed for the Canon Furniture Store. When he reached the downtown area, he parked in a darkened driveway facing the alley. May arrived shortly after, and he backed out of the drive passing the end of the alley in time to see Hollis framed in the back door of the store as he held the door open for May.

He calmly took a drink from the bottle he had stashed in the glove box along with the .22 Ruger in its case. He drove to the car dealership and went into the garage looking around for some very important equipment.

"May, it's good to see you," Hollis said as she came into the office. "I've missed you."

"And I've missed you, too, Hollis. But let's not talk about that. I've got some things to tell you, and I can't talk about the other." May seemed to be struggling to find the right words to convey her feelings.

"What is it, May?"

"I've done nothing but think about us and Martha and Johnny since Beverly found us here last month. I'm sure you've been doing the same thing." Hollis began to say something. "No, Hollis, let me say this, don't interrupt."

"OK, May, go ahead."

"You know that my marriage to Johnny has been a sham since day one. I never should have married him and never would have if I hadn't been pregnant. I just didn't see any other way out at the time. But he never loved me, and I never loved him."

"May, you don't have to. . ."

"Yes, Hollis, I have to. Please, let me finish. When you and I

172

found one another again, I realized I had never loved anyone until just a few months ago. I loved things about people; Johnny's money and car, your status and reputation in town, but I never really loved the person. When Beverly came here that day, I finally woke up."

May paused as her eyes filled with tears. "I realized that I have loved my family, but I had jeopardized everything in order to make myself feel better."

She was sobbing now, and Hollis reached out to hold her, once again in that brotherly manner practiced for years.

"I'm leaving Johnny and Victoria, Hollis. That's why I had to see you tonight. I wanted you to be the first to know," May finally managed to say in one breath.

Hollis nodded his head because he knew she had no other choice. He slowly began to kiss her eyes, nose, neck finally reaching her sweet lips. As they drew together one last time, they held each other tightly and walked over to the couch for their final farewell.

"May, I've always loved you, and I always will. Remember that," he told her as he gently began to unbutton her blouse.

At 8:00, Karen waited just inside the side door on Center Street until she saw Bill walk down the dark block. She opened the door as he approached. Looking both ways before entering and finding the streets deserted, Bill Hoover darted inside.

"She's pregnant!" Karen screamed before the door had a chance to slam shut.

"Sh,sh, Karen, I'm sorry. I just didn't know how to tell you," Bill said contritely. "You know I can't leave her now."

"What about me? I'm pregnant with your child, too, you know. Oh, I can see the headlines now: 'The Great Bill Hoover makes two perfect shots.'"

"Karen, I know you're pregnant. We've got to make some different choices now, don't we? Come on, sit down here and let's talk sensibly. There now, dry your eyes," he soothingly said as he caressed her dark tresses.

"I've looked into a couple of different options, but only one seems workable right now. There's a home up near Traverse City for girls in trouble. They can take you after you finish your exams in a few weeks. You can live there. Now don't worry, I'll take care of all the expenses. When the baby's born in March, they'll find a family who's able to care for it. It's really the best solution."

"Adoption?" Karen asked incredulously.

"Yes, Karen, adoption. You're young and can't possibly raise a child alone, and I owe Alice. We've been married almost seven years, and she's been trying to get pregnant all that time. I can't leave her now," Bill responded in a reasonable tone.

Karen stared listlessly ahead seeing her future change before her eyes. "And after the adoption, what then?" she finally asked.

"Well, you'll have to tell your parents, except maybe you can tell them that some boy at college is the father. After the adoption you can come home and recuperate until fall semester begins. See, you'll only miss one semester of college."

"I see, then what about us?" she asked tonelessly.

"Karen, it hurts me to tell you this because I truly care about you, but we won't be able to see each other again. I've got to devote myself to Alice. Do you understand?"

"Yes, I understand," she responded dully. "But did you know that you were the first one? Did you know that I loved you?" she whispered.

"I knew. I'm sorry, Karen. I really cared. Are you going to be all right?"

"Yes," came the one word reply.

Bill Hoover leaned over and kissed Karen softly on the cheek and then let himself out of the side door of the building after once again checking the street.

Karen lay down on the couch and began softly sobbing until her entire body shook. After a few moments she fell into a fitful sleep exhausted by all of the spent emotions.

Hollis and May stood looking at one another in the middle of the office after both had finished dressing.

"Are you sure, May?" Hollis finally asked after a long moment of silence.

174

"I'm sure."

Johnny came back from the dealership and parked the car behind the supermarket wall which jutted out slightly into the alley. He went to the truck and pulled out a gallon of gas and a butane torch. Before heading toward the furniture store he took one last swig of his powerful medicine.

CHAPTER TWENTY–EIGHT

Beverly and James were returning to Victoria on Thanksgiving night feeling very satisfied and content. Mrs. Kelly had outdone herself, and Beverly had felt safe and secure for the first time in months. Beverly hated to go home, but knew she had no choice.

As they drove through town and past the store, Beverly looked down the street toward the alley and saw smoke billowing out the back.

"Stop, James, stop. What's that smoke?" She asked as James pulled over to the curb across the street from the store.

"Looks like a fire," he said.

Just then they saw Bill Hoover's car drive past pulling into the fire station behind town hall across the street. They watched as Hoover ran inside the building.

"Canon Furniture Store's on fire," he yelled to the volunteers on duty as he came through the door.

The fire trucks came barreling out of the station and drove the one block to the store. They pulled hoses off the two trucks and began hooking up to the fire hydrant on the curb.

James pulled the car over to the curb just past the store. As James and Beverly ran over to see what was happening, they bumped into Hollis and May who were coming from around behind the building. Beverly looked at them in disgust which turned to horror when she turned back to look at the century–old building now filled with smoke.

"He did it, he did it!" Hollis began screaming and pointing at James. "He did it, he hates us and has wanted to hurt us any chance he could. He tried just beating up Beverly, but when that didn't work, he set my place on fire."

"Hollis, please, stop," May pleaded as Hollis continued to scream and point the finger at James.

"Stop it, Dad. James has been with me all night, and you shouldn't go pointing your finger at anyone. What were you doing here tonight, anyway?"

"He's brainwashed you, Beverly. I told you he was no good!"

The street was beginning to fill with people since the fire alarm had sounded almost five minutes ago. The townspeople of Victoria found more than a fire when they arrived downtown that evening.

When the police officers arrived, Hollis started anew.

"Arrest him, Pete. He started this fire. He's trying to ruin me. You know he's not like us; he'd do anything."

"Hollis, calm down. We're not arresting anyone right now."

James stood defiantly on the sidewalk with Beverly at his side.

Bill Hoover looked all around the area and saw no sign of Karen. He quietly went up to one of the firemen and told him there was a possibility that someone was still in the showroom area.

He watched wordlessly as they axed the door, smoke billowing out in huge clouds as they made their way inside. Soon one of them came out carrying an unconscious girl in his arms.

By this time the ambulance staff had arrived and worked over the body of Karen for several silent moments. Then one of them went to the back of the ambulance for a sheet and returned to cover the still and lifeless form.

When the news was brought to Pete Stanhope, the police officer at the scene, he asked Hollis who might have been inside.

"No one, Pete. I was here by myself tonight. Why?"

"Well, Hollis, they've just pulled out a young girl from the showroom. She's dead," Pete quietly informed him.

"Dead? A young girl?" Hollis seemed stunned as he walked around to the side with Pete.

They pulled back the sheet for Hollis to identify the body, and his gasp was audible several feet away.

"It's Karen! What was she doing here?"

177

Bill Hoover watched silently from the sidelines. Then he shook his head sadly and headed back to his car. Beverly nudged James when she spotted Coach walking back to his car.

"Wonder what he's doing here?" Beverly asked.

Hollis came around to where James, Beverly, and May still stood. "Well, now you can add murder to your resume, you son of a bitch! You killed Karen!" Hollis tried to reach up for James's neck, but James was too tall and too strong for him.

"I've had enough of you, old man. Beverly, I'm out of here. Do you want to come?"

Beverly looked from James to her father and then at the store which was nearly engulfed in flames. "Let's go," she finally said and then grabbed James' arm as they walked to the car.

"How can you let him leave like that, Pete? You know as well as me that he's guilty. He's a woman beater, arsonist, and now a murderer," Hollis screamed above the roar of the crowd and fire engines.

"Hollis, calm down. We don't know anything at this point," came Pete's reply.

One of the firemen came from the back of the building to announce that they had the fire under control in the back and thought they could prevent it from spreading down the block.

"And Officer Stanhope? We found something interesting behind the building. Could you come back there with me?"

"Excuse me, Hollis. I'll be right back. Just keep calm," Pete commanded.

James and Beverly could still hear Hollis' shouts as they made their way to the car.

"James, take me back to your mother's house, please," Beverly pleaded.

"Why do you want to do that?" he demanded.

"I feel safe with her, and she'll help us understand what's just happened. Please?"

"OK, but your father. . ."

"I know, honey. He's terrible accusing you when he had been

178

in the back with my aunt. It's awful. And then Karen. Did you see Coach leave?" She tried to divert his attention from the awful things her father had said to him.

"Do you think he'd been inside with Karen?" James seemed momentarily distracted.

"Maybe, I don't know. Why else would he be down there on Thanksgiving night without his pregnant wife?"

They were silent for a few moments before James started pounding the steering wheel. "Damn your family!" he finally yelled.

"I know, I know. Let's just get to your house, James."

He turned to look at her as if for the first time. "Why do I put up with you? You've caused me nothing but grief," he said as he pulled off the main road onto a dirt one.

"Please, James, let's just get to your mother," she cried.

He stopped the car and raised his arm up to hit her.

"James, don't do what your father did, please. You're better than that!" she screamed.

He stopped mid–air. "What do you mean? What do you know about my father?"

"Your mother told me. He used to beat her and even caused a miscarriage the night he left. You're not like him."

James stared at her for a long moment. "My mother talked to you about my father?"

"Yes, and she'll talk to you about him, if you'll just go to her now," she pleaded.

He started the car and pulled back onto the road leading to Ravens Wood Lake. The mention of his father acted as a tranquilizer on the suddenly calm James.

When Pete Stanhope came back to the front of the store, Hollis started anew with his demands that they go and arrest James. May pleaded with him to shut up.

"Hollis, we're not going to arrest James Kelly," Pete announced when he could get a word in between Hollis' tirade.

"And why not? Has he brainwashed you, too?"

"Mrs. Randall, we need to speak to you for a moment," Pete

179

Patricia C. Behnke

said to May, trying his best to ignore Hollis.

"Go ahead, you can talk in front of my brother–in–law," May instructed.

"Well, they called me out back to show me something. We found what we think is the cause of the fire."

"And?" May asked, becoming more and more concerned.

"Well, Mrs. Randall, we found a gas can and butane torch outside your husband's Lincoln parked behind the supermarket," Pete said delicately.

"My husband? Johnny? Where is he? Why is his car there?" May couldn't comprehend what the officer might mean.

"Johnny Randall is in his car. With a bullet through his head. I'm sorry, Mrs. Randall."

CHAPTER TWENTY–NINE

1980 – Ann Arbor

"Wow!" Danny exclaimed when Beverly finished the story. "I understand you so much better now." He gave her a long hug and kissed the top of her head.

"What do you mean?"

"Well, for one, I understand why you act like you hate your parents, particularly your father. They seem like such sweet folks, and I could never understand why you treated them so horribly. I also understand why sometimes you seem almost afraid of me when I'm angry about something. Most of all I now see why you pull away from me mentally at times." Danny shook his head and rubbed his eyes.

"What happened to May? How come no one ever mentions her?" Danny finally asked.

"No one knows. She left town right afterwards. JJ held a small service for his father, but May never showed. I never asked, and the whole family acts like she just died or something."

"Does your mother know. . ."

"No, she's just upset that May didn't fulfill her public duties as Johnny's wife," Beverly interjected before he could ask the question.

"What happened to you and James?"

"We went to his mother's that night. She thought we should stop seeing one another. She didn't see how we could do each other any good. She talked to James about his father. And I agreed with Mrs. Kelly. There would always be a part of James who hated and resented me. When I left my father standing on the street that night, I knew I could stand up to James, too. Then James announced he was transferring to Chelsea for the rest of the year."

"Did he go to Iowa?"

181

"No, never. He played for Eastern, but he never achieved anything like he had in high school. I heard he'd been coaching for a few years. I still keep in touch with Mrs. Kelly. I honestly I don't know what I'd have done without her, Danny. I really want you to meet her; she's anxious to meet you, too, you know."

"I'd like that, but did James ever marry?"

"No, but he still sees Sally."

"No kidding. What about Coach Hoover?"

"As far as I know he's still doing the same thing. He walked away without a scratch, or should I say, burn." Beverly smiled wryly. "I forgot to tell you that the autopsy showed that Karen was about five months pregnant when she died."

"Beverly, you know you have to testify," he said very quietly.

"I, what? What do you mean?" Beverly eyes grew large with fear.

"You must tell what you know about James. He can't get away with it."

"But I'm the reason he did all that stuff. If I hadn't gotten involved with him he wouldn't be so angry," came her defensive reply.

"That's a bunch of bull, Beverly. You don't have that much power over another person. What James did, he did himself, and now he's almost killed a girl! He might get help if he's convicted; otherwise he'll just go out and do it again and maybe this time he'll do even more harm."

Beverly knew that Danny made sense, but she wasn't yet sure that she believed it.

"Beverly, one last thing. You need to put the whole nightmare to rest so we can go on with our lives. You can't do that until you confront it. This could be the way to do it," Danny cajoled.

Beverly decided that first she would talk to her good friend to ask for advice.

"Mrs. Kelly, it's Beverly," she said when James' mother answered the phone.

182

"Listen, I know it's a bad time, but the prosecution against James has contacted my father to ask if I'd testify against James. Danny, my boyfriend, thinks I should, but I can't make that kind of decision without talking to you first," Beverly said in one breath.

"Beverly, you know I've never defended James' behavior. I don't know what he did or didn't do to this girl, but you've got to follow your heart. If you do that, I'll be right behind you. I love you like a daughter, but I was never happier for you then when you stopped loving my son."

"Thank you. I love you the same way," she said before hanging up the phone.

Beverly picked up the telephone once again and slowly dialed her parents' house in Victoria. When her father answered, she told him to go ahead and have Chuck Ward contact her.

The day before her court appearance, Beverly made a surprise visit to her parents. They had planned to go to court the next day for moral support, as they put it. She didn't want them there.

"I'd rather you didn't come to court," she told them.

"But we want to be there for you," her mother said.

"Danny will be there."

"I just want to see him get his due, that's all," her father remarked.

She gave him a long hard look, and then took a deep breath.

"Mom, did you ever wonder why Dad and Aunt May were the first ones at the fire?" Beverly asked.

"Don't you. . ." Hollis started.

"No, don't you. You've been accusing and throwing stones for too long. It's time you had to face some truths, too, Hollis," Beverly interrupted.

"Why are you calling your father 'Hollis'?" Martha inanely asked.

"That's not important. Just ask him why he and May were the first ones at the fire."

Martha looked at her husband who hung his head and refused to answer.

183

"Beverly. . ." Martha began.

"Mom, I hate to do this to you, but your husband and sister were having an affair while I was seeing James. Hollis will need to fill in the details about how long and when. I caught them together a few weeks before the fire. And then that night they both came running out of the back together. Why do you think Johnny burned down the store?"

Martha looked at her daughter as if for the first time. "You are insane. Leave this house right now. How dare you? How did I ever give birth to a daughter like you?"

"Martha, leave her alone. It's true. That's why May left. She came to tell me good–bye Thanksgiving night. She was so ashamed that Beverly had caught us together. Beverly's telling the truth."

The courtroom was packed the day Beverly was set to testify. This trial had received its fair share of publicity and had attracted some interest, but today the whole of Victoria turned out to see what Beverly would say about James.

The prosecutor took Beverly through some routine questions about how she and James had met, what type of relationship they had, and how long it lasted.

"Did James Kelly ever hit you, Beverly?" the prosecutor asked gently.

"Yes," came the barely audible reply.

"How many times?"

"I can't remember exactly, numerous times though."

"What provoked these attacks?"

"My family many times. They treated James horribly while we dated." Beverly finally managed to look at James who sat with his arms crossed over his chest glaring at Beverly.

"What do you mean?"

"Well, they didn't like him because he was black although they never came out and said that. They told me he was bad for me. It would make James angry when someone in my family did something worse than what he had done. Except no one judged their actions."

"Did he ever beat you up? I mean, did he ever do more than just hit you?"

"Yes, once he beat me up quite badly. We had gone to a National Basketball Tournament where the coach from Iowa State had come to watch James play. After one of the games, James heard the head coach talking with Coach Hoover," Beverly paused to point to Bill Hoover sitting in the front row behind James.

"He overheard them talking about making a deal so James would leave Victoria and me alone. The coach from Iowa didn't care much about what Hoover wanted, he just wanted James, but James overheard my father's name mentioned in connection with getting him out of town," Beverly stopped and waited for the next question.

"James took his anger out on you?"

Beverly nodded.

"Please answer 'yes' or 'no', Miss Canon," the judge advised.

"Yes," came the soft reply.

"Was he angry with Coach Hoover as well?"

"Yes. Coach Hoover would lecture him about seeing me and would encourage him to date girls from Ravens Woods Lake; in other words, black girls. He didn't have any respect for the Coach. You see, we saw Coach and Karen Adams leave school together late one afternoon. Only it wasn't just a ride home because Karen hid once she got in the car."

"Karen Adams was the girl who died in the Canon Furniture Store fire."

"Objection, your Honor. This line of questioning has nothing to do with the case on trail," the defense interrupted.

"Your Honor, I'm simply trying to establish that Mr. Kelly has a previous record of becoming angry and taking that anger out on others," the prosecutor countered.

"Objection denied. Continue," the judge responded.

"Yes, Karen Adams died in the fire at the furniture store.

"And didn't your father blame the fire on James?"

"Yes. No one bothered to wonder why it was Coach Hoover

185

who reported the fire. It was also Coach Hoover who told the firemen that Karen was inside. And Karen was five months pregnant at the time of her death."

"What about your father's accusations?"

"Well, he lost his mind that night and kept screaming that James had set the fire. James and I finally left."

"Did James ever rape you?"

Beverly was visibly shaken at this question and waited a long moment before responding. "It wasn't really rape."

"What do you mean?"

"Well, we'd been intimate for awhile and one night when he was drunk he came to where I was babysitting and forced me to have sex with him, but I didn't really try to stop him." Beverly's voice had gotten weaker and weaker as she continued her answer.

"Do you think James Kelly is capable of committing the crime for which he is accused?"

"Objection," the defense again interjected.

"Sustained," came the judge's reply.

"I have no further questions for this witness, Your Honor," the prosecutor said addressing the bench.

"Defense?"

"We have no questions for this witness, Your Honor."

"Ms. Canon, you may step down."

Beverly stepped down from the witness stand. James watched her leave, and when she walked by him, he gave her a slight nod and wave like years ago when he was a star on the basketball court, and she was his best fan in the stands. When she walked past Coach Hoover she gave him a disdainful look. His red face looked like it might explode. Then she noticed Sally sitting right behind James with her head held high. Beverly smiled at her, glad that James had someone to support him. She walked right into Danny's waiting arms and embrace, and she knew that the nightmare had finally ended.

The next week Mrs. Kelly called to tell Beverly that James had been found guilty, but the judge had suspended the sentence in lieu of 100 hours of community service and entrance into an alcohol rehabilitation program. James would never be able to coach basketball again. But he did have Sally and a chance at a better life.

"And Beverly? He wanted me to tell you that he understands why you testified. I told him about your parents, too. And he wanted me to tell you and Danny, congratulations," Mrs. Kelly told her.

"Thank you, I needed to hear that he understood. You know my dad has left town?"

"No, where did he go?"

"To Chicago. He thinks that's where May went. The funeral home is up for sale. Mrs. Kelly, since I don't have anyone to walk me down the aisle at my wedding, I was wondering if you would do the honors?"

"Honey, you sure do like to keep things stirred up, don't ya? Well, I'd be honored. Just tell me where and when." She chuckled.

"First United Methodist Church of Victoria on May 10th, how about that?" Beverly laughed with glee.

"I'll be there, but you better prepare your family. Also, Bev, have you been reading about Coach Hoover?"

"Yes, I have. It's about time some of those girls started coming forward about him," Beverly responded.

The week after her testimony about Karen and Coach Hoover, at least five young woman had come forward to say that Coach Hoover had used his position to seduce them while they had worked for him as an office aide. Charges hadn't been filed yet, but Principal Meyer had relieved him of his duties at Victoria High School.

"I think that bit of news made James the happiest," Mrs. Kelly said before ending the conversation.

On May 10th, Beverly walked down the aisle of the Methodist Church escorted by Mrs. Kelly. Beverly had kept her escort's name a secret from everyone but her mother and Danny.

Martha Canon, who had suffered the greatest humiliation of all, never batted an eye when Beverly told her. Her husband's departure and her sister's defection, had changed her. Beverly and she had even become closer in the last few months as decisions were made about the business. In fact, she even went shopping with Mrs. Kelly to help her pick out the prettiest dress possible for the occasion.

Beverly looked down the long aisle toward Danny, and then turned to give her mother a small wink. To the rest of the congregation she gave her best smile, ignoring the flaring nostrils of those who had never yet experienced a Victorian kind of justice.

About the Author

"Patricia C. Behnke resides near High Springs, Florida on twenty acres with her husband and daughter. However, she lived in Michigan for the first twenty-eight years of her life which gave her ample opportunity to view northern values and lifestyles which she has incorporated into her first novel, *A Victorian Justice*. For the last sixteen years she has taught high school English and writing courses. In addition to writing fiction, she writes human interest pieces for local newspapers."